47 Destinies

By Marlies Schmudlach Perez

Acknowledgements

This book is dedicated to my family, friends
and first readers that offered me advice and showered
me with encouragement: Karl, Heidi, Sarah, Kelly,
Millicent, Thomas, Melanie, Audrey, Francis, Rachel,
Hillary, Megan, Lisa and Frank.

And a special thank you to Matt (aka "Mike") Powers
for introducing me to my publisher, Silverlake eBooks
and Stephen Brailo for giving me the opportunity to
publish my book.

Cover designed by Karl Schmudlach.

http://www.marliesperez.blogspot.com
https://twitter.com/MarliesSPerez

47 Destinies

"Love is our true destiny. We do not find the meaning of life by ourselves alone – we find it with another."
                                                            -T. Merton

Chapter 1

The moon peaked through the leaves of the oak tree basking a dim filtered light upon her face.

"I've been looking for you, my love," he said as he came out of the shadows. She couldn't see his face, but her heart somehow knew him.

"I've been waiting for you," she said, as Cora put her small soft hand into his. He took his index finger and sweetly traced the edge of her beautiful face.

"You have a rare beauty that radiates from the inside out. I have never known such a deep love as I feel for you, Cora," he said, pulling her close to him. He caressed her lovingly and smoothed the wayward hairs from her face. She smiled as he continued to express his heart to her. She finally knew love. She had found everything she wanted.

"I will always know love because I have known you," Cora said, as he took her into a passionate kiss. His arms encircled her as if claiming her. She knew he wanted more, much more. His hand moved down from her hair and sweetly touched her lips. He whispered compliments about her sexy body and pure beauty. His strong hand slowly brushed the inner skin of her arm as their fingers locked together. His gaze stayed firm on her eyes as he penetrated directly into her soul. He was beyond sexy. Cora's mouth was dry in anticipation. He was very clear about what would happen next. She had no doubt. He was ready. She was ready. He…

Beep! Cora's alarm clock harshly jarred her out of dream. Cora smacked at it like an annoying mosquito. She closed her eyes in an attempt to recreate the moment, but it had already passed. Why was her dream world better than her real life? Who was that man?

"Please let it be Saturday," Cora said out loud to herself. The soft sheets cradled Cora's body and begged her to stay in bed. Why was getting up such a chore? She had already hit the snooze button twice. Could she afford a third? Even the alluring smell of coffee from the kitchen didn't entice her. Life felt plain and predictable, and she was horny. Nevertheless, if she didn't get out of bed, she was going to be late for work.

Cora jumped out of bed, got ready and began her drive to work. She was an intern at Locke Incorporated now for a little less than a year. The focus of Locke Incorporated was to build environmentally friendly structures. The green economy was growing rapidly and Cora was very interested in the field. After she graduated in the winter session with her MBA, she began work at Locke Incorporated. The northern office was located in Santa Rosa, which was not far from Cora's apartment in Berkeley.

Cora enjoyed making the drive from Berkeley to Santa Rosa. Driving brought her a feeling of newness,

—

adventure and opportunity. She wasn't sure how she felt about the subject of past lives, but if she did believe in them, she was surely once a dog. When the weather was nice, she would pop her head out of any window available, even a sunroof, if she was fortunate enough to be riding in a car with one. It was exhilarating to feel the air beat against her face. She would let her arm go with the wind and it would dance around and around completely out of control. There was freedom in movement.

Cora was strikingly beautiful. Her long black hair framed her oval face nicely. Her skin was flawless and remarkably soft. Cora wasn't short, but she needed to wear good-sized heels in order to tower over someone. Her sweetness flowed out of her like a gentle downhill stream. Yet when she was angry, you didn't want to be within miles of her. Her blue eyes could penetrate right through you. Her tongue was quick to speak, sometimes without any filters. Cora reacted more than she responded. She was a young woman in her late twenties ready to rid the world of all injustice. Cora was often so focused on helping save the world that she spent little time examining the contents of her heart. She was never short on passion; at least passion for the earth and those in it.

The bright blue October sky brought joy into Cora's heart. It was Wednesday and the weekend was within reach. Her main project was to assist her supervisor with an upcoming conference. The conference in San Diego was a month away. Her role was to assist with details at the location and finish preparing the materials for the workshops and speakers.

Cora's supervisor, Julie, was the true definition of quirky personified. Her hair looked a little like Einstein's, but she knew how to dress and carry herself. Julie was the clown of the office. Her jokes were borderline inappropriate, but often very funny. She gave Cora complete independence, but would also help her sort out any issues when needed. It was a great working relationship.

Cora was relaxed with all of her co-workers. It was a small and friendly office so it was easy to get to know each other. The only person she had not met was Brent Locke. He was an environmental engineer and had his Professional Engineer license. Cora wasn't quite sure of his title, but knew he was Julie's boss and held a strong presence in the newly emerging field of green jobs. California had always been progressive in the green movement and with all the new laws involving green initiatives; the company had no shortage of work.

Cora secretly hoped to never have to meet Brent. He sounded frightening. She heard staff whispering about his abrupt nature. Brent's reputation for being direct was well known in the workplace. Nevertheless, he was highly respected and with this respect came a healthy fear of disappointing him. He traveled a lot so he was rarely in the office. Cora was happy with this fact.

When Cora entered the office, she sensed the buzz of activity. Cora wasn't sure what was happening. Just when she started to settle into the day's routine, the startling introduction occurred. Brent swept briskly into the office. His demeanor was in serious business mode; he was on a mission. His jet-black hair was perfectly in place. His height added to his intimidation factor. His eyes were piercing and stone cold.

He approached her desk and practically barked at her, "Who are you?"

She peered up from her papers and nervously told him, "uh Cora."

He stared at her, said nothing, walked to his office and shut the door.

"Well that went well," Cora muttered under her breath. She wanted to be swallowed up by the carpet; she was so embarrassed.

He was dressed professionally in a suit that went well with his finely groomed hair as she sat in her cheap oversized hand me downs. She couldn't afford much since her paycheck was a measly stipend given to the interns. Even if she had money, she wouldn't have bothered much with her clothing.

A few minutes after the train wreck introduction, Julie came over to Cora's desk. "Have you had a chance to meet Brent this morning? He just flew in yesterday from a meeting down in the Los Angeles area."

Julie beamed whenever she talked about Brent. They appeared close from the conversations Julie shared with Cora; however, after just meeting him, Cora wondered if he was capable of being close to anyone.

"We met." Cora didn't have the heart to tell Julie her true opinion of Brent. "He seemed to be in quite a rush."

It was an understatement, but Cora couldn't think of anything else to say. She wanted to say he was rude, scary, and unfriendly, but she bit her tongue. Her tongue had a mind of its' own and if she didn't literally bite it at times, it often got her in a lot of trouble.

"Well, he is a very busy man. If he asks you to do something for him, be sure to drop everything and help him out. We are a team here. Got it?" Julie sternly stated.

"Of course. I understand," Cora quickly replied.

A team? Really? Wasn't Brent the captain of the dictatorship and everyone else was his royal subject? She realized she was taking it a bit far; however, she had experience with men like Brent. Since they were handsome, they thought only of themselves. They felt women should naturally fall all over themselves to please them. While he was attractive, his abrupt personality was a total turn off.

Cora did not see Brent again until late in the day. His office door remained shut. She could hear his voice occasionally when he was on the phone or in a meeting. Julie bounced in and out of his office all day; each time with huge smile on her face. It baffled Cora that Julie could be so easily drawn into his trap. Powerful men carried such influence over most women. Cora wouldn't be one to bow down to Mr. Brent Locke.

"What was your name again?" Brent said, startling her. She didn't have a chance to spit it out before Brent spoke again. "I need ten copies of this packet. Place them on my desk within an hour," Brent barked at her like a drill sergeant.

By the time Cora recovered herself, he was already back in his office. She didn't even have a chance to make it clear that she wasn't a secretary. She had a master's degree and a ton of other work to do. Cora considered going to Julie to clear it all up, yet she knew it was no use. It was a team environment at the office: Brent's team. She clearly understood that she was the most dispensable member of the team so she got busy with the copies.

When she was finished, Cora didn't take the copies to Brent's office immediately. She waited anxiously at her desk until she was certain he was out of his office. Cora couldn't concentrate on her work so she made a long string of paperclips that reached the floor by the time she was finished. At last, he exited his office. She heard Julie mention a meeting he needed to attend. Maybe he would be gone for the rest of the day; she could always hope.

Cora grabbed the stack of papers and entered Brent's office. It was perfectly ordered. Unlike most offices, there were no papers scattered across his desk. Everything had a precise place and that was exactly where it stayed. The office was very masculine. A large executive desk sat in the middle of the room positioned slightly back from the door. Two wooden antique chairs were placed in front of the desk for visitors. A decent size conference table encompassed the majority of the right side of the office; enough to sit eight people comfortably. Bookshelves lined the wall on the left side from floor to ceiling. It was like walking into a library. The man was obviously fond of books. Four large windows brought the outside in; two windows were behind the desk and two by the conference table. The office carried a distinctly masculine scent. Cora wasn't sure if this was her imagination or from some incense recently burned. It was exactly as she pictured it. Classy. Masculine. Cold.

Cora placed the copied papers in the middle of Brent's desk. Sitting on his desk was a framed picture of Brent with two children; a boy and a girl. The children were under five years old. What surprised Cora was the expression on Brent's face. He was smiling as he squeezed the little ones close. He seemingly loved those children. It warmed Cora's heart slightly to see that he at least was capable of a smile.

Since she had the time, Cora walked over to his bookshelves. She was curious what a man like Brent would read. It was not shocking to see books on business, leadership, management, finances, and success littering the shelves. What did catch her eye were the books on spirituality, love and relationships. She just couldn't see Brent having a softer side. Those books must have belonged to someone else, maybe his wife or girlfriend.

A mound of popsicle sticks in an arrangement that only

the little artist would understand sat on one of the shelves. It was a pile of sticks, glue and crayon marks. Cora carefully picked it up to examine it a little closer.

"Do you always make yourself at home in your boss' office?" Brent stated as he walked up behind her. Cora froze when she heard his voice.

"Um, I thought you were in a meeting?" Her voice squeaked as it came out.

"Nice attempt at deflection! Don't you think that it is rude to be snooping around someone's office?" If she didn't know better, she could have sworn she saw Brent smirk as he gave her the third degree.

Cora put down the popsicle art, literally bolted out of Brent's office and ran outside. What a jerk! He had the nerve to call her rude; talk about irony. He was the king of rudeness. Cora walked around outside to compose herself. After about ten minutes, she gathered what was left of her pride and re-entered the office. If anyone noticed her abrupt exit, they didn't say anything. Brent's office door was closed once again. Cora put in her ear buds and threw herself into her work. She was not going to let him see her unnerved. She was a young yet capable woman; she had dealt with much worse than Brent. At the end of the day, Julie came over to talk to Cora.

"Hey, are you alright? You look pretty stressed out," Julie said as she looked inquisitively at Cora.

"Don't worry. It's nothing I can't handle."

"Good. On a different note, Brent said he got a chance to know you a little better this afternoon."

Cora held her breath. "Oh really? What did he say?" She tried to calm her shaky voice.

Julie responded, "I didn't really understand it; something about you being right at home."

Cora was beyond irritated, but she did her best not to show it. "I have no idea what he is talking about," Cora responded coolly.

"Oh, okay. Have a great night; maybe you will get lucky on your date tonight."

"I doubt it," Cora halfheartedly responded as she dashed out the door.

By the time she reached her apartment, Cora had simmered down about Brent's barbaric behavior. She moved her focus to her date with Josh that evening. Cora and Josh had been seeing each other for about six months. They were friends for five years before moving into the world of dating. They met when Cora was in graduate school through a mutual friend.

Josh was good looking, almost six feet tall with sandy blond hair. He was about seven years older than Cora, but the age difference was not noticeable. The muscles he possessed were all located in his arms. His physical strength was a turn on. He didn't play many sports, but enjoyed hiking, backpacking and horseback riding.

Cora and Josh bonded over their love of music and their long talks about pretty much everything. They loved to share little tidbits from their days, speculate over the weather and spar over politics. They also shared a few mutual friends so it was pertinent to catch each other up on the latest news.

Josh grew up in Montana, which officially made him a cowboy in Cora's eyes. Anyone that comes from Montana was automatically a cowboy; she told him this all the time. Cora was fascinated with how Montana was so rural and filled with what she called 'farm animals'.

Cora was content with Josh. He was fun to be around and they shared things in common. They had been friends for so long that their friendship naturally progressed into something more. There was never a falling-head-over-heels moment for her, but in a way she was glad. She had plenty of experience with that emotion; it always all started out so great and then very quickly the rose-colored glasses would come off.

She wanted something real this time. She wanted a relationship that could go the distance. Cora was tired of heartbreak and wasting precious time on dead end relationships. Josh had seen her through her fair share of break-ups before they began dating. He sat through cartons of ice cream and countless boxes of tissues. Josh was reliable and straightforward; there was no guesswork and no unwelcome surprises. Their relationship wasn't a passionate romance, or very romantic at all. It was safe, comfortable and exactly what Cora wanted.

Josh came over to Cora's apartment after work with bags of take-out. Cora enjoyed any food, which came out of a box or bag. After exchanging the standard pleasantries, Josh told Cora about a conversation he had with his mother that afternoon.

"A few cattle broke through the fence which borders our neighbor's dairy farm this morning. My dad had to take the truck and bring them back to the ranch. My mom said it has happened three times this month," Josh said as his brow furrowed with concern.

"Cows dominate Montana; the ratio is three cows to every one person," Cora reminded Josh. "It is doubtful that anyone actually has a firm count on all the cows. There could be a ton hiding up in all those Montana country mountains," Cora gleefully smirked.

"City girl, you haven't even been to Montana so how do you know?" Josh enjoyed teasing Cora. He tried unsuccessfully on several occasions to bring Cora to his hometown. He wanted her to experience the life he once led; unbeknownst to Cora, the life he intended to return to before long.

"I've seen plenty of pictures," Cora said without much interest.

"Internet pictures and scenes from Brokeback Mountain don't count."

"I'm fine right here surrounded by people. At least you can talk to people. Who do you talk to out there? The cows?" Cora giggled. Knowing Josh, he probably did talk to the cows, the fence posts or anything for that matter. He was a talker.

"No, I don't talk to the cows. Well, not often that is," Josh scooped Cora up in his arms and twirled her around. He loved her playful spirit. She was so compassionate, loving and fun to be around.

"You brute. Put me down," Cora playfully squealed.

"No," Josh said.

"Excuse me?" Cora responded.

"Not until you agree to come with me to Montana next month."

"I can't. I have the conference next month," Cora was happy to have such a viable excuse.

"No problem. We will go right after the conference. It is the week of Thanksgiving."

Cora did not anticipate Josh's valid comeback to her flimsy excuse. She was stuck in a corner.

"I may not be able to get the time off from work," Cora tried fumbling for an excuse.

"I am sure Julie can manage without you for one week." Josh knew he was wearing her down.

"Can I get back to you?" It was her last attempt to

avoid the inevitable.

"No. I want an answer right now." He had her exactly where he wanted her. He wasn't going to give up.

"Geez, Josh. Why are you being so stubborn? This is unlike you," Cora wasn't used to him being so persistent. He was usually fairly passive.

"Stop avoiding the topic at hand."

"Okay. I will ask Julie if I can go, but if she says no, I won't be able to go."

"Great. When are you going to talk to Julie?"

"I will talk to her tomorrow," Cora said knowing she had lost.

Once again, her gut told her she was settling for what the man wanted in the relationship. Cora couldn't understand Josh's love of the wild. She enjoyed being outdoors, but she did want to be within at least a few miles of another person. However, she understood that in every relationship, compromise was important. Of course, she would rather compromise on where they went to dinner instead of where they spent their vacation time.

Afraid of disrupting their comfortable relationship, Cora kept it to herself. It just all felt a little fast for her. Going to Montana meant meeting Josh's family and meant some type of commitment, yet they weren't even lovers yet.

———

Cora also wasn't sure she was ready for all of the inevitable questions that would come up about her relationship with Josh. How serious were they? What were their plans for the future? Even though they had known each other for years, their time together dating was all relatively new. She was still sorting through a lot of the answers herself. They had a few serious issues that they hadn't discussed like where each of their individual dreams was taking them. Josh talked non-stop about Montana. What if he wanted to move there? Cora loved the Bay Area and had no desire to leave.

Ugh. There she went again straight to fear. It was just a visit to Montana. She wasn't signing up for the military or having brain surgery. She really needed to chill out and take a breath. After all, it was Josh. Cora felt safe around him. He wouldn't let anything happen to her. If his family was as great as he was always bragging about, there was nothing to worry about.

As expected, Julie was more than happy to give Cora the time off. Cora tried to come up with reasons she was needed at the office, but Julie would hear none of it.

"Montana. Have you ever been? I heard it is incredibly beautiful," Julie gushed after giving her enthusiastic blessing to Cora's request. "And, just what will you be doing in Montana?"

"Just hanging out, I guess."

"Is that all? Is there anything you need to tell me? Come on, don't hold back," Julie prodded in her nosy way. It irritated Cora to no end.

"No. It is just a simple trip home for Josh. He wanted me to tag along."

"Geez. You are so guarded. Won't you give me any details?"

"There are no details to give," Cora truthfully responded.

"So you two still haven't been *intimate* yet?" Julie emphasized the word intimate and stretched it out way further than it needed to be.

"Stop it! A little tact please! Everyone can hear you." Cora was blushing terribly.

"What tact? Julie? You obviously don't know Julie very well," Brent said with a laugh as he rounded the corner. He had on a deep blue blazer that matched his hazel eyes perfectly.

Brent's Cheshire cat grin was evidence that he overheard Julie's question about Cora and Josh's sex life; or lack of one in this case. Cora couldn't believe her dumb luck. If there was an embarrassing moment at hand, Brent was sure to be there to witness it. Brent had the ability to grate on her last nerve and at the same time shoot bolts of energy straight through her body. This man was trouble and upsetting her comfortable world.

Chapter 2

Saturday came faster than Cora expected. Work picked up a ton since the conference she was assigned to work was fast approaching. Cora was so busy that she was able to avoid Brent without much effort. She practically fell into her bed on Friday night. She had a date with Josh to go to San Francisco for the day and he would be over in the morning. Luckily, she remembered to set her alarm before her head hit the pillow.

In her dream, Cora heard knocking on her front door. When it didn't stop, Cora jolted out of bed and grabbed the alarm clock. It was 9am. Cora panicked. She accidentally set the alarm clock for 6pm instead of 6am.

"I'm coming," Cora yelled out as she ran to the door.

"I am sorry, Josh. I set my alarm clock wrong. Just give me ten minutes and I will be ready."

"No worries. Take your time," Josh said as he took a seat on the couch and flipped on the TV.

Cora hopped into the shower and quickly scrubbed down. Cora noticed that Josh did not offer her a kiss when he met her at the door. Why didn't he make a move? Maybe he wasn't attracted to her. They had kissed, but not much else. Rejection didn't sit well with her so she chose to just stay silent.

Cora was true to her word and ready in ten minutes. By then Josh was fully engaged in a Saturday morning cartoon. When Josh got into a TV program, it was difficult to get his attention. Cora took her time and had a bowl of cereal and a yogurt. She plopped herself next to Josh on the couch so at least he would know she was ready.

"I'm ready. Josh? Hello, Earth to Josh," Cora said tugging on his ear.

"I...um...yes?" Josh was clearly distracted.

"Did you still want to go on our date today?"

"Oh, yes...of course. Let's go," Josh slowly got up to turn off the TV. Even though the first cartoon was over, he had already begun a new one. Josh was a TV addict, especially when it came to cartoons and sports. She wasn't certain, but Cora was pretty sure all guys entered their 'man cone of silence' when watching a baseball or football game while possessively gripping the remote control.

"Let's go," repeated Josh.

"You already said that," Cora said, standing near the door.

"I did? Sorry." Josh tucked his tail between his legs as

they left. He knew she was irritated with what Cora called his 'immature love of cartoons'. Great, now he was going to sulk for a bit. Relationships are difficult, thought Cora.

"I'll drive," Josh called out as they headed toward the street.

Josh steered his Toyota truck onto Highway 80 and headed toward the city.

"So, where are we going?" Cora asked trying to get excited about their day. So far the start of their date fell pretty flat.

"You'll see."

As they approached Oakland, Josh exited the highway. "Are you stopping for gas?" Cora wondered aloud.

"Nope."

"I thought we were going to the city."

"We are."

"Are you going to tell me anything?" Cora's voice started to take on a higher pitch as the conversation wore on. She was getting nowhere and not very happy about it.

"Nope," answered Josh.

"Fine." Cora folded her arms around her chest and

decided she might as well stop since she was getting nowhere - except worked up. She wanted to take in the fine scenery, but the Oakland freeway view didn't offer much of that. As they drove on, they ended up near the bay. It was an incredibly beautiful day. The fog had already burnt off and the sun was coming through the few white clouds that still hung around.

"We're here. Hop on out, we only have a few minutes to spare," Josh proudly announced.

Cora opened her door and gazed up at the Blue and Gold Fleet ferry terminal. Their boat was docked and passengers were already boarding. Josh grabbed her hand and started running toward the ticket office.

"Two round trip tickets please," Josh blurted hurriedly to the customer service representative.

"You've just made it. Present your tickets to the gentleman at the gate. Better hurry. The ferry waits for no one," the representative told Josh as he slipped his credit card back into his wallet.

"You heard the lady. Our ferry awaits," Josh said in a goofy theatrical voice trying to mimic the ticket agent.

They were the last passengers on the ferry. It started to move as they roamed around searching for some seats. It was Saturday, so there were plenty of seats available since the normal commuters were all at home. The weekend passengers mainly consisted of families, young adults and a few couples. They made the 10:40am ferry, so they had 35 minutes to enjoy the ride until they reached the Ferry Building in San Francisco. A maximum capacity sign read that it could hold 350 passengers. There were three decks accessible to the public. Cora dragged Josh to the upper deck so they could have a view of the city. The breeze was slightly chilly outside; however, it was forecasted to be a warm October day and the sun was starting to feel really nice.

The noise created by the water slapping against the boat combined with the engine was louder than Cora expected. It wasn't the best situation for an engaging conversation, not that she wanted to have one anyway. She wanted to just sit back and enjoy the ride.

Cora's long black hair couldn't resist tumbling with the wind created by the boat. Every once in a while it flew in her face, but it mostly stayed at her back. The air felt sensational against her skin. It brought back that feeling of freedom. It was intoxicating. Cora bubbled with excitement when she saw the Bay Bridge coming into view. The ferry skirted around Angel Island before it darted under the Bridge. The view from underneath the bridge helped Cora gauge its enormous presence. She was excited to be able to share this experience with Josh. Cora was sure he could feel the energy it all created.

"Isn't the bridge incredible?" Cora belted out above the noise.

"What?"

"The bridge," Cora said as she looked over at Josh. His head was buried in his new cell phone.

"Oh, the bridge. Yes. It looks crowded today," Josh said still fixated on his phone.

Cora tried to push down her annoyance of his cell phone use. He obviously was not able to experience this moment with her. They could talk more about it later she thoughtfully reasoned.

She walked over to the rail so she could feel the spray of the water mixed with the rays of the sun on her hands and face. It took no time for her to re-enter the moment. Water. Air. Sky. Sun. It all blended together. She was relaxed. It felt good after such a busy week. She felt stressed lately and she knew exactly why. It had to be Brent. Yet even through her fear and embarrassment, Cora was now realizing she was attracted to him. He carried this innate power in his nature that she had never known. People wanted to be with him. Men wanted to be him. Women wanted to be noticed by him. She had just wanted to stay out of his way. Brent was surely not interested in her.

"Hey, you okay?" Josh startled Cora with his concern.

"Josh, I'm having a great time. Why?"

"You have a frown on your face and you seem upset. Are you unhappy that I took that phone call?" Josh shot back.

"I was just thinking about work. Nothing important," Cora brushed it off. It really wasn't that important. Brent Locke might think he was important, but Cora wasn't going to ruin her day with Josh by giving Brent another ounce of her time.

"You sure? You've been pretty stressed out this last week," Josh said as he finally put away his phone.

"I have? I didn't realize it," said Cora with a bit of a smile.

"I've noticed you've been a little distracted as well," Josh commented.

"I'm just antsy about this upcoming conference. This is the first time I have been working on something on such a large scale. I guess I am just worried that it won't go smoothly. I don't want to let Julie down."

That was it! Right? Wasn't that what stressed her out? It surely had to be. And if it wasn't, she wasn't going to give Brent the satisfaction of knowing that he was catching her off guard.

After the ferry docked in San Francisco, Josh and Cora roamed around the Financial District to view the wares of the street vendors. Josh bought a t-shirt for himself and a headband for Cora. They enjoyed roaming through a farmers market and picked out a few Asian pears. The fall weather was incredible. The fog had fully burned off and the sun was making its way across the sky. The couple continued their walk and headed toward the piers to view the cruise ships. A Carnival cruise ship was in port. Passengers were disembarking for a day trip in the city. Cora and Josh were suddenly surrounded by other actual tourists. It seemed fitting to continue on with the group and act like tourists.

They arrived at Pier 39 and held hands off and on as they browsed through the stores. Pier 39 was a paradise for tourists. The stores catered to visitors: souvenir t-shirts, mugs, sunglasses, fudge, taffy. It was all available. Josh couldn't resist playfully dragging Cora through every store. He put funky sunglasses and bizarre hats on her and he took countless pictures of Cora with his new smart phone. Cora often wondered why they called them smart phones since there was such a steep learning curve for Josh to figure his out. If they were so great, why didn't they come with a smart person to help Josh operate his?

"Smile!"

"You are too much," Cora laughed.

"Come help me pick out a few postcards. Do you like the ones with the Golden Gate Bridge or the panoramic view of the city?"

"Seriously? Who are you going to send a postcard to? We live in the Bay Area," Cora said looking at him strangely.

"Remember. We are tourists today," Josh replied.

"Yes. Tourists."

Josh took the postcards up to the register. The sales clerk proceeded to ring up the purchases.

"Where are you folks from?"

"Montana," Josh said as he tipped his hat in a friendly gesture.

"How long are you visiting San Francisco?"

"Me and my wife will be out for a week and then we need to return to the ranch. The snow will fly before you know it and we'll need to ride those cattle into the barns before they get stuck on the other side of the ridge."

Cora hid behind the rack of postcards. She was barely able to suppress her laughter.

"Make sure you visit Ghirardelli Square. Their chocolate is my favorite," the sales clerk shouted out as they exited the store.

"Wife?" Cora exclaimed.

"Yep. Been married three years now and hopein' a little rancher or ranchetta comes along soon," Josh said in his best cowboy drawl as he smacked Cora's rear.

"Yee haw!" She shouted out with excitement. "You tryin to rustlin' me up Cowboy?"

"You ain't seen nothin yet," Josh said as he flashed Cora a sexy grin and tipped his hat again. Before she knew it, he had literally swept her off her feet and scooped Cora up in his arms. He hugged her tight and then placed her back down on the ground. Right before her breath returned, Josh leaned in and passionately pressed his lips upon hers. His hand moved into her hair as his fingers entwined themselves in her long black mane. His lips moved back and forth slowly across hers before his tongue pushed open her mouth and locked together with hers. Cora felt desire run through her body. Finally, it was happening. Cora was so caught up in this kiss that she forgot they were standing in the middle of Pier 39. Suddenly, her lips were empty and as Cora opened her eyes she realized the moment was over.

"Sorry about that," Josh mumbled as he pulled away.

"Don't be sorry. That was incredible. I've been waiting awhile for that passion to emerge."

"Oh, you have?" Josh said coyly.

"I have and I'd like a little more."

"Now? How about we pick this up when we are alone?" Josh said folding his arms across his chest.

"Fine. If you are embarrassed by a few people staring at us, I guess we can wait." Cora giggled as she realized they had become quite the spectacle.

"Yes, little city girl and soon to be country girl. You need to practice some patience."

"Patience! I've been patient long enough. And speaking of patience, when are we going to get some chocolate?" Cora said as she pouted.

"My little chocolate lover, I know you like the best. Let's go get that need for chocolate met and then we will see about those other needs later."

Luckily, for Cora, Ghirardelli Square was not far away. Cora was in high heaven. The sweet smell of chocolate was teasing her from a block away. They had lunch in the Ghirardelli Café. Cora treated herself to a large chocolate shake and even ordered a small sundae. If she was a tourist on vacation, she was going to act like one. Josh took a picture of her under the large Ghirardelli sign and asked someone to take a picture of them together. Josh put his left arm around her and pulled her tight against him. Josh's fingers brushed against Cora's breast. His hand slid under her jacket and rested above her waist. Before she knew it, he was kissing her again while the stranger continued to take pictures.

"It is great to see young love," the stranger taking the pictures commented. "Are you on your honeymoon?"

"Yes. We got married a week ago," Josh replied before Cora could correct the man.

"My wife and I have been married for 32 years. I still remember our honeymoon to Niagara Falls. Take lots of pictures. You will treasure them in years to come," the man said as he handed the camera back to Josh.

"Thank you. We will." Josh was beaming as the stranger and his wife continued on their way.

"Wow. I have been distracted lately. I didn't even realize we got married last week. I need to pay more attention," Cora laughed with her hands on her hips.

"Next time, will you please notify the bride that the nuptials are taking place?"

"I promise you that next time, you will remember," Josh shyly stated.

"Are you sure?"

"I am positive," Josh said with a hint of confidence.

"Now as for remembering, I distinctly recall that a new wife has some wifely duties she should perform for her new husband. What do you think if we go back to your place and I start fulfilling some of those?" Cora said, ready for the evening to begin.

"Patience. We still have the rest of the day ahead of us. A real tourist would make the most of their surroundings and I intend to do just that."

"Being a tourist is awfully exhausting. Don't you think we should rest somewhere first?" Cora pouted.

"We can't. Not yet," Josh replied as he looked at the map.

"Fine." Cora pretended being cutely upset, but couldn't stay pretend mad as Josh pulled a bar of chocolate from his backpack.

"Are we good?" Josh already knew his answer as Cora delighted in the chocolate slowly melting in her mouth.

"We have a cable car to catch," he said to Cora.

The rest of their day raced by and before they knew it, they were sitting on the ferry headed home. Cora often wondered about time and why it had different speeds. The ride back held a sweet anticipation in the air. They both knew what was about to happen and both were excited.

The car trip back to Cora's place was quiet, notwithstanding the music from the radio. It was Cora's favorite time of the day. There was something spiritual and enchanting about this period of dusk which announced the death of the each day's light and the birth of evening darkness. Everything became more vibrant. The leaves on the trees were quiet as if in prayer. The sky appeared to bend down to the grass to kiss it with beautiful shades of color. All things began to descend into the slow darkness like shadows waiting for the dawn.

Cora's mind was the clearest at this time of the day. She loved poetry and often fell into a dreamy state and pondered her destiny. She would not process the trivialness of the day. She'd move more into the beauty of life and the blessings available to everyone. She felt alone for a few moments and would bathe in the beauty of the solitude. She felt capable of anything and also unable to do anything. It was all so refreshing and peaceful. She wanted to hold on to it so desperately, but knew she could not. For merely pondering life is not living life. True living requires experiencing the all of it; the good and bad. Cora placed these feelings of beauty and peace into her heart. She'd cement the moment in her mind; aware that it too would eventually flee. She wanted to share her thoughts with Josh, but again didn't feel the timing was right.

When they arrived at Cora's apartment, Josh pulled a gentleman's move and opened the car door for her. They felt like teenagers as Cora fiddled with her key in the lock to her apartment. She wasn't sure why she felt jittery. It was Josh, but then it wasn't. Not the Josh she was so comfortable with and had known for years.

What if they weren't sexually compatible? What if he didn't like what he saw? Cora's demons often plagued her before she was intimate with someone new. She wondered if all women struggled with this before revealing their bodies to a man. It was unnerving, yet so exciting. Cora went into the bathroom to compose herself. When she returned to the living room, she noticed two wine glasses and a bottle of Merlot nearby. Josh was occupied finding some music on the radio so Cora sat down on the couch and opened the wine.

"Is Lynn going to be home tonight?" Josh inquired about Cora's roommate.

"No. We have the place to ourselves. Are you ready for some alone time with me?" Cora said hoping Josh hadn't changed his mind.

"Yes, this is perfect. Do you want to come over here?" Josh asked while extending out his hand.

Cora walked over to Josh and handed him his wine glass. Josh took a sip and then set it on a nearby table. The timid Josh from the pier was gone. He took both of his hands and ran them through her hair.

"You have the most beautiful hair. It is like a wild stallion's; so fitting for your personality."

When Cora attempted a response, Josh put his finger to her lips to silence her. He bent down and gently brushed his lips across hers. His hands went from her hair and moved down her back. Both hands paused on her hips. Josh stopped kissing her and just stared deeply at her eyes.

"I've been waiting for this moment for years. I can't believe it is here," Josh said as his fingers skimmed the collar of her blouse.

His fingers brushed softly against the cotton fabric and began to trace the outline of her bra. The anticipation was killing her. She wanted it. He knew she could barely hold herself together. In order to relieve some of her sexual tension, he gently lifted her silk blouse above her head and threw it to the floor. As the music played gently in the background, Josh drew Cora close to him and began a slow seductive dance. His hands and fingers acting as small massagers caressed her hair, and then they moved down her back and to her chest, barely touching her yearning breasts. His head dipped down and he placed small sweet kisses all around her neck and naked shoulders.

Cora finally had enough and unbuttoned her pants. She quickly pushed them off her legs and dragged Josh to the couch. She needed to take control of the situation. At this rate, they would never actually make love. Josh was still completely dressed, but not for long. Cora removed his shirt, practically ripped off his pants and peeled off his boxers. The only clothing left on Josh was his socks. If she weren't so turned on, she would have busted up laughing. He actually looked a little frightened.

Cora roughly pushed him down and made him sit on the couch. She knelt down, placed her head between his legs and gently spread them. Josh groaned in excitement. Turned on that Josh was responding to her dominating lead, Cora firmly grabbed his member in her hands and watched it grow erect. She opened her mouth and slid her tongue around the tip of the head. She went around and around until Josh's moans got her wet. Cora went down on him hard and pumped her head up and down, going faster and faster. Before she knew it, she tasted the warmth of his release in her mouth.

"Oh, that felt so good, Cora," Josh moaned.

"I'm glad you enjoyed it. I am going to clean up and I will be right back," Cora said as she slipped off into the bathroom.

She brushed her teeth and then rummaged through her drawers to find something sexy to wear. She chose some simple lingerie that showed off her legs, but wasn't too slutty. Josh seemed to like the wholesome look. Cora peeked at the mirror as she passed by and quickly freshened up her makeup. She wanted to look perfect. When Cora sauntered back into the living room, Josh's snores greeted her. Cora was disappointed. Now what? Should she wake him or let him sleep? It was not how she planned the evening would end. She was all keyed up and unsure what to do. Was foreplay all he had in mind for the night?

Cora had waited long enough. She wasn't going to let this deter her from getting what she wanted and what she needed. Cora looked like a sweet baby doll in her light pink negligee. White lace trimmed all the edges. It was see-through and went down a little past her hips. It came with white lace panties, but Cora purposefully left those in the drawer. She wore no shoes so her bright pink toenails could be seen. A small gold locket in the shape of a heart lay right above her breasts. If she could say so to herself, she looked pretty damn hot. Staring at the sleeping Josh wasn't getting her anywhere. Cora brushed her hand through his short sandy blond hair. It was course and thick. Josh slowly began to stir. His eyes opened to find Cora straddling him with a huge smile on her face.

"Hey, sleepy head. You ready for round two?" Cora said as she traced her hand over his naked body.

"Am I dreaming? You look incredible. Stand up and let me get a good look at you," Josh said now fully awake.

Cora seductively rose from Josh's lap and paraded herself around the room. She suggestively bent over right in from of him pretending to pick up something meaningless off the floor. She peered back at Josh from a between her legs view.

"Oh! It looks like I forgot to put on my panties," Cora giggled as she shook her butt back and forth.
Josh was already erect and more than ready to give Cora what she wanted. He reached over into his pants pocket and pulled out a condom. His hands shaking, he quickly ripped it out of the wrapper and put in on. Before Cora could stand back up, Josh drove himself into her hard and fast. Cora screamed out. She was taken off guard and was barely wet enough to handle his quick entry. Cora stood up to brace herself for his pounding. Josh grabbed her hips to get a better grip on her body. The rhythmic pounding of his excited member against her created some welcome friction.

Right when Cora began to get into it, Josh turned Cora over and dragged her to the floor. He entered her in the basic missionary position, more gently and manly this time. Cora chose to lie still to give Josh the pleasure he desired. It wasn't long before Josh came again. He collapsed against her, exhausted from the events of the day and the evening pleasure. Cora grabbed a blanket and some pillows off the couch to cover them. Cora nuzzled close to Josh and wondered if sex was mainly for the man. Perhaps cuddling was what the woman gained from the whole experience, she wondered.

The next day, Cora woke up to the sound of Sunday morning cartoons. It wasn't her ideal fantasy, but when she noticed the hot cup of coffee within her reach, she mellowed out. Josh was busy in the kitchen crashing pots and pans together.

"Hey sexy, did you sleep well?" Cora purred as she walked into the kitchen with her coffee.

"I sure did. Out like a light."

"Thanks for the coffee," Cora said as she kissed his cheek.

"I was going to make some breakfast, but all I could find is yogurt, a dried up apple, cereal and expired milk."

"You know I am not that into cooking. Plus, I need to keep this figure looking good," Cora said as she modeled her negligee again.

"You have nothing to worry about sweetheart," Josh said as he grabbed her rear. "You are a little wild in bed. Has anyone ever told you that?"

"I can't say they have," Cora said with a half grin. She had only had sex a few times in her life. It had to be with someone safe that wouldn't hurt her heart and would care about her regardless of how she looked. Even though Josh complimented her body, she still felt unattractive at times. It was a demon she brought with her for many years now. Someday she was going to face it. But for today, she was going to place all her attention on Josh.

Chapter 3

Monday always arrived faster than Cora wanted. The conference was three weeks away. Cora was busier than ever helping Julie with all the details of the event. It was going to be held in San Diego on the Coronado Island at the Hotel del Coronado. The hotel was legendary and the perfect setting for an conference.

This was the 10th year the company hosted the conference. From what she heard, each year it gained more exposure and the attendance increased. This year, already over 300 people had registered. Julie was in charge of the entire event so Cora was right there by her side helping with everything.

It was nearly 7:00pm when Cora finished up her last email to one of the workshop presenters. Julie had already left a half hour earlier to pick up her son from a soccer game. Cora didn't mind working late, but after her weekend with Josh, she was plain worn out. Cora noticed the light was left on in Brent's office. Since she was the last one there, it was her responsibility to ensure the office was closed up properly. When Cora entered Brent's office, she was surprised to see him typing on his computer. She backed up very slowly so he wouldn't notice her.

"Going somewhere?" Brent deviously inquired.

"I didn't know you were in the office. Julie asked me to lock up when I left," Cora said.

"It's dark out. Do you always stay this late?" Brent shifted from his computer screen and placed all his attention on Cora. Her nerves were unsettled as she tried to remain composed.

"I like working when the office is quiet. With the conference fast approaching, I've been putting in a few extra hours. Don't worry, Mr. Locke. I don't make overtime," Cora quickly added.

"Dedication is an important quality to exhibit for an intern. Then again, so is tact."

"Yes, I agree," Cora said as she tried to figure out where the conversation was going.

"Are you ready to go?"

"Yes, I am done for the evening," Cora reminded him. Didn't she already tell him?

"Good. You will join me for dinner. I know you haven't eaten." Brent stared at her fully expecting her only response would be yes, of course!

"I haven't," was all Cora managed to say as her mouth was completely dry. How did this man manage to put the fear of God into her and tick her off at the same time?

"Don't forget to turn off the lights," Brent said as he grabbed his keys off the desk and threw them in his blazer pocket.

While Cora fiddled with the alarm code, she heard Brent start his car. Maybe he was just joking about going to dinner. Deep down, Cora knew that wasn't the case. Her brown slacks and long sleeve blouse suddenly felt very plain. Thank goodness she slipped on a pair of heels before she ran out of the apartment that morning. What in the world would she talk to him about? Where was Julie when she needed her?

Cora reluctantly made her way over to Brent's black Audi. She attempted to put a smile on her face. He was Julie's boss; she at least owed him a friendly face. The car was warm when she opened the door. The scent of lavender washed over her. Cora noticed a bunch of fresh lavender wrapped in brown paper in the back seat. Interesting. Maybe the flowers were for his wife or girlfriend. Cora really knew very little about the man. After careful prodding, Julie told Cora he was around 40, but she wouldn't give any additional details. Cora was still curious about the picture of the little girl and boy on his desk. Maybe she would build up the courage to ask him tonight. They were going to have to talk about something.

"Fish?" Brent said out of the middle of nowhere.

"Excuse me?"

"Do you eat fish?" Brent asked.

"Yes, I do."

That was the extent of their conversation during the 15 minute drive to the restaurant. It was fine with Cora. She was still trying to calm her nerves. She was sitting next to the man that had been stressing her out for weeks and now she was trapped in his car. They were alone and would be for at least another hour. No wonder her head was throbbing.

They arrived at the restaurant and Cora was not surprised to see candles and white tablecloths on the tables. She mentally gave up. She was underdressed, couldn't think of any civil topics to discuss and 100 percent out of her comfort zone. Instead of freaking out, Cora decided to flip her viewpoint and look at the positives. He knew she had no money; just looking at her clothes made that fact evident. So at least she was going to get a free meal out of it. Plus, he wasn't attracted to her so she felt no need to pretend to be a sultry attractive woman. He was simply hungry and he wanted to eat. This reality was bearable. If she could just get over the last mental hurdle that he was drop dead gorgeous.

The restaurant was fairly empty seeing as though it was a Monday night. There was an older couple sitting near the door and a group of four off in the corner. Brent requested the window and they were seated immediately. The maître d referred to Brent as 'Mr. Locke'. Brent obviously frequented the restaurant often to be known by name. After they were seated,

Brent ordered a bottle of Cabernet Sauvignon. It was brought out right away and a small amount was poured into his glass to taste. He nodded his approval and the two glasses were filled.

"Are you old enough to drink?" Brent asked very seriously as he handed her a glass.

"It isn't polite to ask a woman her age, but if you don't believe me, I can show you my driver's license," Cora tartly replied.

"Do I offend you?"

"I find it best to bite my tongue when I am around you, Mr. Locke" Cora admitted.

"You can call me Brent," he replied with a swagger.

"So, Cora please tell me, are you usually nice and relaxed with everyone else except for me?"

"When you put it that way, it sounds pretty bad." Cora already felt the affects of the wine on her empty stomach. She rarely ate breakfast and had skipped lunch that day.

"It is definitely a different and curious approach," Brent said.

"Well since I am already off to a bad start, I guess things can only go up from here," Cora fired back.

"That's one possibility," Brent replied with no emotion.

The waiter rescued Cora for a few minutes when he came to take their order. She wasn't too sure about all the special cooking terms or fancy descriptions, but she understood words like swordfish, halibut and salmon. She just could not ignore the pricey expense listed to the right of each entre, while she was painfully trying to make her selection.

"It's my treat, please order whatever you like," Brent stated over his menu.

Could Brent sense her concern over the high prices and the lack of money in her wallet, Cora questioned to herself? Likely her face gave it away. She tended to squint her beautiful blue eyes, and tighten her lips in a distinct way when she was nervous.

"What brings you to my company?"

"Your company?" Cora's voice was slightly cracking as she questioned his question.

"Technically, it belongs to my father, but since his retirement last month, I run Locke Incorporated now. Have you been to the southern office?"

"No," Cora said.

"It is our business headquarters."

"Is that why you travel so much? I thought you were out reviewing the projects," Cora said as she played with her glass.

"I do some of that as well, but I leave most of that work to the supervising engineers. They need to earn their keep. The duties required of a CEO take the majority of my time."

"I imagine it would," Cora said as she sat with her thoughts. She felt pretty foolish that she was irritated when Brent asked her to make a few copies. Then again, he could have been a little friendlier. No wonder Julie insisted that Cora provide Brent with assistance when requested.

"I probably should move down South, but I enjoy the Bay Area," Brent said more to himself than to Cora.

The rest of the evening passed rather quickly. Cora began to feel slightly comfortable around Brent; as comfortable as anyone could be around such a strong mysterious personality. She learned a lot about Locke Inc., Brent's vision for the company and his views on the field of professional environmental services. It felt like she was sitting in on a board meeting, but she still gave Brent her full attention even when she had no idea what he was talking about. He seemed like he needed someone to talk with, so she lent her ear. As suspected, Brent didn't reveal any personal details about his life outside of work and Cora wasn't about to broach the subject. She was curious about the picture on his desk, but not brave enough to ask. Things were going better than at the beginning of the evening and she wasn't about to press her luck.

After dinner, Brent dropped Cora off back at the office.

———

Brent waited to make sure her car started before he drove off. On her way home, Cora looked at her cell phone and realized that she missed Josh's routine 7:00pm call. She usually kept her cell phone on vibrate during work hours and forgot to turn the ringer back up. It was already close to 10:00pm; too late to call Josh back. It wasn't a big deal. Josh wouldn't care. What did concern Cora was that all her thoughts that evening were absent of Josh until now, as she didn't even remember their nightly ritual until she saw the missed call on her cell phone. Being around Brent was like being caught in an impenetrable force field. She was going to have to be very careful around the man. He wasn't to be trusted. Cora knew it and would surely be on her guard next time.

Cora couldn't wait to see Julie the next day so she could give her a piece of her mind.

"Hey, thanks," Cora said sarcastically to Julie.

"What's got your panties in a bunch? You really need to get Josh in bed so you'll mellow out some."

"Funny. Not that it's any business of yours, but we sealed the deal this weekend."

"Oh, I get it. You are cranky because you are worn out. Nice," Julie congratulated Cora.

"Yes," Cora said without thinking. "I mean no. I am cranky because you were remiss in telling me that Brent is now the CEO of this company. It was kind of a

—

critical detail for you to leave out."

"You're joking, right? You didn't know Brent became the CEO? You really need to leave your desk more often and mingle with other people," Julie playfully counseled Cora.

"Thanks for the compliment, Julie, but I am very dedicated to my job."

"I don't understand why you are upset that Brent is the CEO."

"I made a fool of myself yesterday when I was talking to Brent and I don't like that feeling," Cora admitted.

"Cora, you have to be on your toes around Brent. You seem to always step into it when he is around," Julie said.

"I do. What is it about him?" Cora wondered aloud as she raised an eyebrow.

"Maybe you being uncomfortable around him is actually a little crush in disguise?" Julie inquired.

"Who has a crush?" Brent said as he came up behind Cora.

Julie was now laughing and resisting a response. Cora was bright red and unable to find any words.

"Cat got your tongue, Cora?" Brent said. When she didn't respond, he added. "Hey, I forgot to thank you for keeping me company at dinner last night."

Julie was still laughing and Cora had gone mute so Brent, with a proud of himself smile, gestured he was relenting as he threw his hands in the air and walked back into his office.

"Dinner? Really!? No wonder you are cranky. It's ok. Brent tends to eat pretty late and he likes to drag people along. I should have warned you about that," said Julie as she regained her composure. "So about this crush?"

Cora interrupted, "I do not have any feelings for the man. Period. I also have no intention of developing any. In fact, I plan to stay as far away from him as possible," she bristled as she stomped off.

Julie was now laughing again. However, she wasn't about to burst Cora's bubble and tell her that it was already too late. Cora would have to find that out on her own.

Avoiding Brent was more difficult than expected. He seemed to be everywhere that day. Was she more aware of him because she was attempting to avoid him or did he somehow know that the mere sight of him ticked her off? Didn't he have some meetings to attend? Shouldn't he be at one of the project sites? The southern office must need the man. Instead of keeping to himself, Brent was socializing in the halls, having lunch in the break room and going from desk to desk chatting with staff. Did an alien take over his body? He barely said, "Boo" to most people and yet here he was on top of the world. What was with this guy? He was impossible to figure out. Maybe she was wrong about him. Maybe there was a little boy hiding behind Brent's cold exterior.

"I'm not paying you to daydream Cora," Brent said as he sat down on top of her desk.

"I was calculating the cost of the evening social we are hosting at the conference."

"Nice recovery," responded Brent stated as he clapped his hands.

"Excuse me?"

"You are excused," Brent said as he left her desk. So much for Cora's brief idea that the man had an ounce of a soul. He was cold, selfish and downright rude. There was nothing he could ever do to change Cora's opinion. She needed to find a way to not let him get to her. It was unproductive and foolish to let her boss know that she didn't like him. She was going to have to change her tactics. The sound of Cora's phone beeping jarred her out of her contemplative state. She read a text from Josh.

'Are you okay? You didn't return my call last night.' Great! Now Josh was on her case. She just couldn't catch a break today. Cora texted him back in an attempt to soothe things over.

'All good here. Worked late last night. Will call you tonight.'

———

Hopefully, that would suffice. Cora didn't feel like talking to Josh right now. She was still keyed up. Engaging in another battle didn't interest her at the moment. Her phone beeped again with a text from Josh that read,

'Oh. I was just worried that you were upset because of this weekend.'

Upset? About what? The sex? Or Josh falling asleep after he got his pleasure, thought Cora. She wasn't upset before, but this text conversation was starting to annoy her. Luckily text messages don't display tone because it took Cora a moment to think of a response that did not portray her frustration.

Cora replied back, 'Not upset. Just really busy at work. Enjoyed this weekend.'

That was all Cora could muster up. Her headache from the morning returned with a vengeance and she still had an hour of work left. Cora popped a few aspirin and went back to her work on the conference agenda. Even when irritated, Cora had the remarkable ability to separate her work and personal life. She removed Josh and Brent from her mind completely and threw herself into her work.

Cora's irritation returned on the drive home. She was pretty down in the dumps on the drive and all of a sudden everything became an issue. Her commute sucked. She wasn't paid enough for the level of responsibility they gave her. Nobody appreciated her work. Her car was old and needed repairs that she couldn't afford. Traffic stunk. She had no food at home to cook for dinner yet going out to dinner didn't fit into her ridiculously tight budget. Brent was a pain in the ass. Josh needed to grow a pair of balls. Life seemed to be conspiring against her.

As Cora walked up to her apartment, she tripped on her neighbor's newspaper. Luckily, she caught herself before totally tumbling over. She twisted her foot a little since one of her heels caught in a gap in the sidewalk.

"This perfect day will just not end!" she said out loud to herself.

Upon opening the door to her apartment, Cora thought she smelled Chinese food. Great, now her mind was even against her. The lights were dim and candles lit up the room. A large vase of daisies was in the middle of the kitchen table surrounded by several small white take out containers. Josh was seated at the table.

"You have no idea the day I had," Cora said as she slid into a chair. "I had a massive pity party on the way home. I was getting close to having one of my mini meltdowns and then I find you here ready to save me from myself."

"I felt a little coolness in your text messages and I know work hasn't been easy for you lately. Do you want to talk about it?" offered Josh.

"Thank you so much, I would love to, but first I want to dig into all this food. What did you get? And how did you get in?" Cora asked.

"I called Lynn. She suggested that I order some Chinese food. She left a key for me under the doormat. She said it would cost you a fortune cookie so be sure to save one for her."

"I guess I can do that," Cora said as she winked and shook her hip at Josh.

"We have all of your favorites: beef broccoli, lemon chicken, soup, brown rice and wontons."

"You are the best!" Cora said as she grabbed a box. "My boss' boss is driving me insane! He grates on my last nerve."

"He has no idea who he is messing with. What has he done? Make you work late? Has he threatened to fire you?" Josh asked, a little flippantly Cora thought.

"No, nothing like that."

"Is he rude to Julie?" Josh asked, sounding non-supportive.

"Hardly. She thinks the sun rises and sets on the guy," Cora said in a defeated voice.

"Alright. I am done guessing."

"He says mean things to me," Cora said unsure how to put Brent's actions into words.

Josh didn't want to get caught up in the guessing game again, "Can you provide me with an example?"

"I have tons. I was in his office one day when he was out and I was looking at things on his bookshelves. I saw some popsicle sticks all glued together and it intrigued me. I picked it up to get a better look and he came up behind me and said something about me being nosy."

Josh tried to be helpful and not laugh, but it was no use. He didn't want to hurt Cora's feelings because he could tell she was already bent out of shape. He now second-guessed himself thinking he would have been better off not bringing up the subject when she was still angry, but it was far too late. He suddenly felt he was on the hot seat, when his whole goal of the evening was to get himself out of the doghouse. He wondered if she was on her period but was afraid to ask, and smartly so.

Before he lost it all, he tried to redeem himself. "What else did he say?"

Cora wasn't sure she wanted to proceed. She couldn't tell whose side Josh was taking. For some stupid reason, guys tended to stick up for other guys when they didn't even know the whole situation.

"You know, I rather not talk about it anymore. I am plain worn out about it all. In fact, I am thinking of looking into getting a different internship. My dad was all for me taking this internship, but he wouldn't tell me why. I am sure I can find something closer to home here that makes the same amount of money or more,"

Cora said more to herself than Josh.

Josh was confused. Cora was stoked when she got the position. It was quite a prestigious company that people strived to work for and would do almost anything to be a part of. She beat out a great deal of competition for the internship. Interning with the company was one of the only ways to get a foot in the door.

"Let's talk about something less volatile. How is Lynn doing? I haven't seen much of her these days," Josh said kindly.

Cora gladly accepted Josh's way out of the conversation. She was surprised to hear herself say that she might look for another job. It was the first time she even thought of quitting. She tended to get wound up like a top and a spin out of control. But if Brent kept it up, maybe she would move on. He better watch himself.

Josh and Cora finished out a relaxing evening. They watched a movie Josh rented and called it a night. Cora was physically and emotionally worn out. It was unlike her to bring work stress home. She needed to resolve this tension with Brent. She just wasn't sure how.

Chapter 4

The rest of the weeks leading up to the conference flew by. Cora did a fairly good job staying out of Brent's way. Overall, it was easy since he spent the majority of those weeks in the southern office. Julie and Cora were right on task and even ahead of schedule in some of the planning areas. The idea of quitting left Cora's mind completely. She thoroughly enjoyed interacting with the conference speakers and getting to know them. The theme of the conference was "Making Environmental Design Through Green Building Options Workable."

It was the night before Cora and Julie were flying down to San Diego when it all came apart. Cora was packing some of the clothes Julie lent her when her cell phone rang.

"Cora? It's Julie," Julie said between sobs.

"Julie? What happened? Are you alright?"

"No. Yes. I don't know. I am just worked up. I was at my son's soccer game this afternoon. He was playing really well. Anyway, one of the players slid right into him and broke his leg. We are at the hospital right now. I've already called Brent. He assured me that the conference would be handled without me. I really need to stay with my family. I hope you understand."

Understand? There was no way Cora could pull off the conference without Julie, she thought. It was her first trip to San Diego, let alone her first conference with the company. The news was terrible, but she didn't want Julie to feel any worse than she must have already felt.

"Ok, hopefully Brent is right. We will do our best to handle it. Please don't worry. Your family comes first," Cora said trying to sound confident and reassuring to Julie.

"Cora, I know you can do it. If you need anything, please call me. Okay?"

"Of course, take care of your son and don't worry about a thing."

"Thank you," Julie said with noticeable relief in her voice.

Cora hung up the phone and was completely numb. Brent told Julie that 'we can handle it.' Cora wondered about Brent's definition of 'we'. To Cora's knowledge, Julie and she were the only ones actively involved in the conference. Maybe someone from the southern office was going to help. She wouldn't panic until she knew more. It didn't take long for Cora to learn more. Cora's cell phone rang again.

"Cora?"

Cora didn't recognize the incoming number. "Yes, this is Cora Jacobs." If it was a telemarketer, she was going to give them a piece of her mind.

"This is Brent. Julie can't make it to the conference. She has a family emergency."

"Yes, I know I just got off the phone with Julie and heard the sad news about her son. Who will take Julie's place in running the conference?" Cora asked already planning how she could assist them and update them on the details.

"Nobody. You are now the lead," Brent confidently stated.

"Me?" Cora responded in a whisper.

"Julie said you know every detail and can handle it."

"She did?" Cora was about to throw up.

"Was she wrong? If so, I need to know right now," Brent demanded.

"No, I can handle it," Cora said totally unsure of her abilities.

"I will meet you at the Hotel del Coronado tomorrow to make sure everything is ready to go. I will call you on this phone when I arrive," Brent said as he hung up the phone.

"Okay." Cora wasn't sure if he heard her response before he hung up. He didn't even ask her if she wanted to do it. She was about to save this man and his conference, and he couldn't think of one nice thing to say to her. A simple 'thank you' would have been nice. While highly annoying, she had bigger problems on her hands. This was the first conference Cora helped organize. However, she knew every detail inside and out. She had all of the notes, schedules and details with her already. It wasn't going to be easy, but she vowed she was going to make it happen.

Cora's flight to San Diego the next morning was uneventful. There were not a lot of passengers flying on a Sunday morning. It was the second to last week in November. She spent the time rereading the list of things she needed to do. Registration began the next evening so Cora had time to put everything together before then. The conference would last a total of five days. The first day was mainly for travel and registration. The bulk of the event was Tuesday through Friday. The agenda was packed with workshops and main sessions. The total pre-registered list was now up to over 500 attendees. Julie said a few more always register on-site, but it would only be a handful. Cora's nerves began to resurface as the plane landed. Would she be able to handle this?

After picking up her luggage, Cora looked for a driver holding up Julie's name. Julie had the foresight to arrange for a town car to take them to the hotel. Cora was very thankful. It would have been a hassle for her to rent a car and try to find Coronado Island on her own. The day already had enough stress without adding getting lost to the list.

San Diego was simply beautiful in the fall. Cora heard it was usually perfect weather no matter what time of year. It was her first time in San Diego and she planned to enjoy as much as the conference would allow. The sun was out and there wasn't a cloud in the sky. People were walking around in shorts. It was in the low 70's. The scenery was luscious. Palm trees grew like tall weeds. Tropical flowers lined the streets. Cora lived most of her life in the Bay Area surrounded by fog, breezes and cool weather. It was surprising to see people walking around in summer clothing so late in the year. Summer, or the perfect illusion of summer, evoked specific images in her mind. The beach, perfect sun-kissed weather, little quaint sea towns, people basking in the slow roll happiness can bring; it was all a part of summer. San Diego seemed to offer that summer feel year round. Cora was an instant fan.

Crossing over the Coronado Bridge was breath taking. Boats littered the bay. Coronado Island was, in fact, a peninsula connected by a long thin piece of beach. There were relatively few tall buildings on the island, and from what Cora could tell, the Hotel del Coronado was the only beachside hotel. Cora did not know much about The Del. She heard it was historical, but it was a mystery to her. When the driver pulled up to the main entrance, Cora let out a gasp.

"It gets me every time," the driver said.

"I've never seen anything like it."

"The intricacies are all over The Del. You will no doubt enjoy your stay," the driver said proudly.

"Oh yes, things are beginning to look a little better than I expected," Cora said with a huge smile on her face.

"Maybe if you are lucky, you will see Kate Morgan," the cab driver said with a smirk.

"Who?

"You don't know the story of Kate Morgan?"

"I don't. Please tell me," Cora insisted.

"Back in 1892, Kate Morgan came by herself to stay at The Del. She was married to a man named Thomas Morgan. They were con artists who made their living swindling passengers out of money during card games on the train. Kate had long black hair and was very attractive, quite like yourself."

"Thank you," Cora said as she blushed. "How old was she?"

"I think twenty-seven."

"That's how old I am!"

"Kate was pregnant and wanted out of the swindling business. Her husband was not happy about the baby or leaving this way of life. Kate got off the train in San Diego and her husband was to meet her at The Del days later to celebrate Thanksgiving together. Rumor has it, a few days into her stay she went into town and purchased a pistol and seashells. When her husband did not show at Thanksgiving, she shot herself in the head on some stairs which led to the beach," the driver said, lost in the story.

"Kate must have been terribly distraught over her husband to take her own life and the life of her unborn baby," Cora said sadly.

"Some claim it was not a suicide. The coroner's report says the bullet in her head did not come from her pistol. It came from a different gun. The report also stated that the position of her body was not one caused by suicide. There are people that claim it was foul play, perhaps even her disgruntled husband."

"How intriguing!"

"Since her death, many sightings have occurred in the hotel. People have seen her in the hallways, windows and there are many reports of strange things occurring in her room, 3312. The curtains move when there is no breeze, a green glow comes from the windows and maids have reported objects floating in the air. The room remains closed to guests; however, The Del opens it on Halloween."

"Thank you so much for sharing this story with me. It adds more mystery to an already enchanting wooden castle."

"Have a great stay, Miss," the driver said as he opened

her door.

"Thank you. Have a nice day," Cora said as she tipped the man and stepped out of the car.

Cora couldn't believe that she would be staying at The Del for an entire week. It was truly a work of art. It was difficult to describe; it was unlike anything she had ever seen. The talent of the craftsmen that designed and built The Del was revealed in each feature. The love they had for their craft showed through all the small details that made it so unique. The red turrets stood proudly with flags on the top waving in the wind. Everything but the roof was white: the numerous porches, balconies, landings, windows, gutters and siding. It was like a Victorian castle.

As Cora walked up the main entrance, she felt a sense of importance wash over her. Every aspect of The Del breathed luxury. The two-story lobby was covered in a dark wood; perhaps cherry or walnut. Intricate carvings and the placement of the wooden beams accented the glorious room. The second story boasted of a balcony area where guests could spend hours taking in the splendor and perhaps some gossip. A round wooden table was positioned precisely in the middle of the lobby. On the table was an enormous vase filled with an arrangement of lilies, long stemmed roses and other fragrant flowers. Above the table was the most magnificent chandelier. Cora couldn't take her eyes off of it. Each little glass piece sparkled and shined. Ropes of crystals were strewn together and reached up in a semi-circle to cover the lower half. Large lights that looked like crystal buttercups were situated on three separate brass circles with each ring getting smaller as it moved to the top. Over 26 buttercup lights sat upon the brass rings. Ropes of crystals hung off each light like elegant icicles.

Cora chose to stay in the Victorian Building. It was the original historical part of the hotel. She didn't want the modern; she wanted to experience the richness of The Del's history. Maybe she would even catch a glimpse of Kate if she was lucky. Of course, there wouldn't be much time for exploration with the conference close at hand, but she would get in as much as possible. Cora checked in and took the elevator to her room. The elevator was made with long brass bars which contained space between each bar which made the elevator transparent. The elevator shaft had the same openness, so when it moved, a fresh breeze entered. The historic elevator required a uniformed operator who was very friendly and manually opened the elevator door for Cora once she reached the 3rd floor.

Her room was beyond anything she imagined. A queen sized bed with a huge walnut headboard was decorated with lavish pillows, shams and linens. Cora couldn't resist jumping on top of the bed as the softness enveloped her. Classic wooden nightstands stood guard on each side of the bed. White crown molding kissed the edges of the ceiling and made its way to the floor. White wicker shutters opened for a view of the ocean. It was simply heavenly. Cora fell in love with the room and wished she could marry her bed.

"I am one lucky girl," Cora said out loud to herself.

Cora unpacked and changed. Julie lent her several very elegant dresses and even a few suits. She knew Cora didn't have the money to purchase the clothes she needed for the week's events. In light of the fact that Cora was now running the conference, she was extra thankful. Maybe if she looked the part, she might feel more confident. After freshening up, Cora got down to business. She pulled out her various checklists and began going through each item one-by-one. She met with the hotel's conference manager for a few hours.

The manager took Cora on a tour of the meeting rooms, banquet halls, pools, restaurants, gym and even the spa. Cora wanted to know the place inside and out so she could help the attendees with any of their needs. The manager took her to Garden Room where the company dinner would occur on Tuesday evening, the area on the beach where the Friday evening luau would be held and the Crown Room where the main sessions of the conference would commence. Everything was absolutely perfect. She could see why the company chose the location each year. She couldn't imagine anything being better. After her meetings wrapped up and the details were all in order, Cora took a stroll out to the beach. She found a nice bench at the edge of the sidewalk and the start of the sand. It was the perfect place to take it all in.

No matter how many times she gazed upon the ocean, she was spellbound by its splendor. Cora found so many thoughts to play with when she came to the ocean. She felt the grandeur at the ocean that is available to all that seek it; everyone is welcome there and all walks of life are drawn to it. She wondered, does the rhythmic sound take us back to the memory of swimming in our mother's womb? Is it the warmth of the sun that brings us a calming sensation? Could it be the sand between our toes that draws us to our childlike nature? Is it the vastness of the sea that stirs within us the realm of all that is possible? Or does it all swirl together and become something which we cannot name or describe, but simply feel and be. Cora knew that not everything had to have a rigid definition or understanding. The feelings of the heart can sing a song to the soul that is not audible to the human ear.

It was captivating. The sun loomed above the horizon, still hours from making a plummet into the water. It burst forth orange rays that captured laughter and happy voices and spread them everywhere. Little children frolicked in the water as anxious parents loomed closely with towels. Dogs barked at the sand crabs and sloshed around in the foam in search of floating tennis balls. Lovers strolled hand-in-hand along the sand that was wet by the last wave. Surfboards bobbed between the waves in wait for something big enough to lure them away from the peaceful lull of the sea.

"Quite remarkable, isn't it?" Brent said as he took a seat next to Cora.

"Honestly, why are you always sneaking up on me?"

"Always?" Brent said with a devious smile. "Do I frighten you, Cora?"

"Yes, you do," Cora figured the truth was easier than

coming up with some vague lie he would see right through.

"Ha. You haven't seen anything yet," Brent said throwing his head back in laughter.

"That isn't very reassuring."

"I am not here to reassure you, Cora."

"Trust me, I know," Cora said tersely. "How did you find me?"

"It was pretty easy. I am staying in the villa right behind you."

Cora turned around and saw a beautiful modern villa with the classic red roof of The Del. It must have contained four or five bedrooms. Why he needed so much space for one person was beyond her.

"Let's go have a drink before dinner," Brent said as he got up from the bench. The man definitely did not know how to politely ask for anything. However, he was certainly good at demanding things. Cora didn't feel like there was an easy way for her to say no, so she followed Brent. She wasn't exactly sure where they were going for a drink. And dinner? Did the man have a fear about eating alone? Ugh, another dinner with him? She wasn't sure her nerves could handle it with all the stress of the conference looming.

Pushing aside her concerns, Cora followed Brent into his villa and was stunned by the beauty. The entire room was right out of a Coastal Living magazine. Cora had to close her mouth as it had literally dropped open.

"Keep your hands to yourself," Brent said laughing as the words came out of his mouth.

"I wasn't touching anything," Cora said defensively.

"Yet," Brent shot back.

Brent poured two glasses of wine without asking Cora what she wanted to drink. She bit back a rude comment for once and accepted the glass. Brent sat down on one of the numerous white sofas. Cora followed suit and positioned herself with a view of the ocean. It was difficult to be anxious surrounded by such elegance. They sat quietly for a few minutes and neither seemed to mind.

Cora took the time to study Brent a little. He looked a bit more approachable in the relaxed setting. It was the first time Cora saw him dressed slightly more casually. He wore khakis and a white linen shirt. He even smiled. Thank goodness Cora changed outfits before leaving for the earlier meetings. She wore a long brown dress appropriate for an evening out. For once, she fit in with her surroundings. Cora caught Brent looking her up and down. He was probably glad that her clothing wouldn't embarrass him. Cora didn't realize it, but the dress accented her slim body and showed off her curvy hips and her firm buttocks. Her black hair draped nicely down her back. She was a hidden beauty; this reality hidden only from Cora and nobody else. Men secretly admired Cora's hourglass figure. Julie knew exactly what she was doing when she picked out Cora's clothes for the week. Julie knew what caught a man's eye and purposefully lent Cora clothes that accented Cora's best features. Cora often caught men staring at her chest. It frustrated her, so she would stare back, maintain eye contact and force them to act like gentlemen.

"Let's go," Brent said, once again startling Cora. "Are you usually this jumpy?"

"No, I can't say that I am," Cora responded.

"I won't bite you."

"Promise?"

"I don't make promises I can't keep," Brent said with a wicked smile.

Cora had no idea what that meant, but decided against prodding any further.

They left the hotel villa and walked down the street. Teenage boys passed them with surf boards in hand discussing wave heights and past surfing stories. Girlfriends paused to peer in shop windows chatting about the latest fashions and the cute dresses calling out to them. Mothers pushed strollers about as they corralled little ones away from the street. Restaurants spilled out along the sidewalks as tantalizing smells allured the patrons into the vacant seats. Tables adorning white cloths held classy matching plates. Silverware clinked on the plates and glasses, adding a sweet music into the air. People lounged in wrought iron chairs sporting wine glasses and other exotic concoctions dreamed up by the bartender. Conversation was the main course. Laughter permeated everything. Warm air was slowly being pushed away with the coming of night. Solitary candles shone proudly, adding ambiance to the mood.

They walked to the restaurant in silence. What neither of them noticed, is that they made a striking couple. Brent was a good half foot taller than Cora, even with her heels on. They each carried themselves with a quiet confidence and solitary strength. After passing many restaurants, Brent stopped at the Chez Loma French Bistro. The restaurant resided in an old historical house that had a ton of charm laced with class.

"We're having French food," Brent said as he opened the door for Cora.

"Thank you," Cora responded timidly. Cora's words either ran out of her mouth or completely dried up around Brent. There was no middle ground.

After they were seated and two new glasses of wine were poured, Cora began to open up.

"Have you been here before?" Cora asked as she admired the décor.

"Yes, it is my favorite restaurant on the island."

"I can see why. I feel like I have died and gone to heaven. Everything on this island is simply remarkable," Cora gushed as she popped another shrimp in her mouth. "I may not go back."

"I don't think they hire interns at this restaurant."

"Funny. I actually have some valuable work skills."

"I am counting on it. I need this conference to go off without a hitch. Why else would I be feeding you?"

"It will. I have no doubts," Cora firmly stated.

"A little confident, are we?"

"You're one to talk. Mr. Confident himself."

"If you have it, use it," Brent said as he refilled Cora's glass. "Don't look now, but you seem to be relaxing around me, Cora. You know that is when I am the most dangerous."

"It's the affect of the wine. I doubt, however, that I will ever completely relax around you," Cora said, matching Brent's stare.

"Good. A smart woman stays on her toes. She should never give up her edge."

"Why is that?" Cora asked.

"When she gives up her edge, she loses some of her attractiveness."

"Are you saying I am attractive?" Cora wondered eager

for his reply.

"Are you putting words in my mouth?"

"Are you avoiding my question?" Cora said, refusing to give in to his attempt to avoid the question.

"Do you think you are attractive?" Brent said, turning it back to her.

"What?"

"Do you think you are attractive?"

"That wasn't the question I asked you," Cora said with a slight pout.

"Answer mine and I will answer yours."

"My boyfriend thinks I am," Cora said defensively.

"Ah yes, I recall hearing a little about him back at the office."

Avoiding his response, Cora shot back, "I answered yours, now you have to answer mine."

"No, you avoided my question, so I, in turn will avoid yours," Brent volleyed back at her.

"Are you always this difficult?"

"Yes. Do you have any other questions for me?" Brent asked assertively.

"You have a picture of two young children on your desk. Who are they?"

"That is a very private question," Brent said unwilling to answer.

"Do you have a very private answer?"

"Yes, I do."

"And?" Cora knew she was really pushing it, but the wine was getting the best of her.

"I will tell you, but not tonight," Brent said as he looked away.

"So you are going to tell me, but I have to wait. I have to say, it is not the answer I was expecting. Then again, I didn't really think you would tell me. You appear to be a very private person."

"There are good reasons for my privacy."

"Care to share any of them?"

"No," Brent said, not willing to budge an inch. "Tell me more about your boyfriend."

"Fine. What do you want to know?"

"Whatever you are willing to tell," Brent said, smirking.

"Josh and I met in college. We started out as good

friends. We began dating a few months ago." Cora had no idea what to tell Brent. Talking to him about Josh made her uncomfortable and she still wasn't sure why.

"Do you love him?" Brent said, staring intently at her.

"You just go right to the heart of an issue."

"Do you?" Brent smugly persisted.

"Honestly, I don't know," Cora said truthfully. "I am not really sure what it means to love someone."

"Have you ever been in love?"

"I am sure I have at some level," Cora said, looking down at her napkin.

"What does love mean to you?"

"This is not the type of conversation I would expect to have with you, Brent."

"You sure have your avoidance technique mastered. How about you practice the technique of answering questions?" Brent said staring intently at her.

"You're one to talk."

"You cannot master a master, Cora."

Cora was so defensive around Brent. He was truly demanding. She was used to getting her way with guys.

Not Brent. She knew she needed to change her tactics with him, but it wasn't working. He was her boss; she needed to keep that in mind.

"Want me to repeat the question?" Brent said. "You look completely lost over there."

"I am not sure why these questions are so tough for me to answer," Cora confessed.

"Maybe you've never really experienced love and so you cannot describe it."

"I've had my heart broken a few times."

"Do tell," Brent said intrigued by her admission.

"I will tell you, but not tonight," Cora said with a huge smile on her face.

"Good one. Let's get out of here."

After they finished dinner, they walked through the little town of Coronado. They moved in the direction of the setting sun in order to enjoy the beautiful colors it left behind in the sky. They passed through neighborhoods lined with charming homes with carpets of green lawn, flowers and various decorative fences. She often wondered what it would be like to live somewhere else. Cora could envision herself living in any house and pondered where she would work, what her neighbors would be like, if she was in love; she could fully immerse herself in the imaginary life. She was fascinated with the concept of stepping into someone else's shoes. Would their life bring her more fulfillment? Feeling into someone else's destiny helped her keep her mind off her own.

"You are awfully quiet over there. Care to share your thoughts?" Brent asked after walking in silence for awhile.

"I was just thinking," Cora said, locking her fingers together behind her back.

"I figured as much. What about?"

"I was wondering what it would feel like to live inside someone else's body."

"I don't understand," Brent said as he stopped walking to listen to Cora.

"If my soul was placed in another body, would I still be myself? Would my destiny still be the same?"

"Good question. I've never thought about it."

"What really makes up 'me'? My body? My spirit? My soul? Is one more powerful than the other? Is there a difference between a spirit and a soul?" Cora wondered out loud.

Brent was quiet for a bit. Cora was feeling stupid for opening her mouth. She had so many random thoughts and around Brent she couldn't seem to keep them to herself.

"I'm sorry, I tend to ramble," Cora said slightly embarrassed.

"I didn't realize you had such depth. You are full of surprises," Brent said, as he began walking again.

"You have no idea. Maybe I am related to Kate."

"Kate Morgan?" Brent asked.

"You've heard of her," Cora said, once again surprised by his attention to detail.

"Cora, everyone that has been to Coronado Island knows the legend of Kate Morgan. She is more popular than all the royalty, presidents and Hollywood stars which have stayed at The Del. Of course, none of them died here so she has that on them."

"What do you think of the theory that she was murdered?"

"It is possible. Perhaps the hotel did not want their guests knowing that a murder occurred at The Del. It would have been bad for business. Maybe the police made it look like a suicide; that would explain the inconsistencies in the coroner's report."

"It sounds like you are a fan of Kate's."

"What's not to like about her? She was a hot con artist," Brent said as he laughed. "In fact, you do resemble her."

"We were both 27 when we stayed here," Cora offered in order to keep the conversation going.

"And you both have long black hair."

"And…." Cora said, fishing for a compliment.

"Are you pregnant?" Brent said in a fit of laughter.

"No!"

"You sure?"

"Not funny, Brent," Cora could not get a read on this man.

"I think that is where the similarities end. That is, unless you are moonlighting as a card shark. I better watch you around my wallet," Brent said, as he ruffled Cora's hair.

It would not have hurt Brent to tell Cora that she was also attractive, Cora thought. One minute she thought Brent was interested in her and the next she didn't. At any rate, Josh was looking better and better by the minute. He was simple. You knew what he thought and what he would do. Wasn't that what Cora wanted? Someone practical. Mystery was overrated.

When they arrived back at The Del, Cora tried to part from Brent.

"I will see you tomorrow. Thanks for dinner," Cora said when they arrived near Brent's villa.

"Where is your room, Cora?"

"I am staying in the Victorian Building."

"I will walk you to your room," Brent said as he put his arm through hers.

"That isn't necessary."

"It wasn't a request. Who knows, Kate might be out and about looking for one of her relatives."

They walked through the outdoor restaurant and into the lobby. People were everywhere. Brent recognized a few of the conference participants and stopped to say hello. Cora felt awkward standing next to Brent when he failed to introduce her. If he would have just let her walk by herself, she would have been spared some embarrassment. She almost walked off a few times, but reminded herself that Brent was her boss. It was becoming her new mantra, 'Brent is my boss. I must respect him.' So far it was only halfway working. She understood he was her boss, but the respect part was not an easy pill to swallow.

"What floor are you on?" Brent said when they finally made it through the lobby.

"Third."

He didn't ask if she wanted to take the stairs or the

elevator and simply proceeded to the stairs. They walked up together in silence. When they reached the third floor, Cora led Brent to her room. As she slipped the door key in the slot, Brent said good night and was gone in a flash. Cora was thankful that she didn't have to invite him in. Her room was a mess. She didn't spend the time to put away her clothes and the bed was a mess from her earlier dive into the pillows. Cora pondered the strange mannerisms of her boss. He was outright rude at times but he also had gentlemanly manners. He opened every door for her, held her chair for her when being seated and even made sure she arrived safely to her room. He was surely not a normal man. Quite frankly, she wasn't sure about him at all. While she sat on her bed thinking about Brent's characteristics, her phone rang.

"Hello?" Cora said half in a daze.

"Are you okay?" Josh said with a little worry in his voice.

"I'm fine. Why?"

"I've been calling you all afternoon and evening, and I couldn't reach you."

"I'm sorry. I left my phone in my room. I had meetings with the hotel's conference manager. This place is incredible!"

Cora was resistant to tell Josh that she had so far spent the majority of her time having drinks, dinner and conversation with Brent. She didn't want Josh to think something was going on with her and Brent, as that was surely not the case. Nevertheless, since there was nothing going on, then why didn't she want to tell him? It was perplexing. Maybe her conference nerves were getting the best of her.

"Are you all ready for tomorrow?" Josh said. He understood her anxiety.

"I hope so. There is a lot of pressure on me to do well."

"You will be fine. Call me if you need a pep talk," Josh offered.

"Thanks. I will. Good night."

"Good night."

It took Cora awhile to go to sleep. She was energized. In her mind, she kept replaying her conversation with Brent; she felt so foolish. Why couldn't she keep her mouth shut? She questioned her boundaries and the filters between her head and her choice of words. Did she really ask him if he thought she was attractive? Unbelievable. She had a boyfriend. She wasn't interested in Brent. And even if she was, Brent was her boss.

As Cora lay in bed, she swore that she heard some moaning. Ghosts stories tended to go right to her head. It was likely the creaking of the wooden floorboards. What was Kate's room the cab driver told her? Cora remembered that it was 3312. It was only a few doors down from hers. Cora couldn't resist the temptation to walk near it. Since it was late at night, there were no guests in the hallway. Cora put on her coat and stepped out of her room. When she approached Kate's room, her heartbeat slowed considerably. Cora felt a wave of pure sadness wash over her. It was like Cora could feel Kate's energy inside her body. There was no light coming from under Kate's door. Cora put her hand on the door knob and felt a jolt of energy pass right through her. It freaked Cora out and she ran back to her room. She dove into bed. Cora's heart was pounding. Why was she messing around with such dangerous things? Brent. Kate. Was Cora simply losing her mind?

Chapter 5

Cora was more than ready to get up the next morning. She had a full day ahead of her. She had a lot to prove and was ready to take it on. She dressed and then caught a quick breakfast. It was Monday, and the conference registration began at noon. Two employees from the southern office were arriving at 11:30am to receive instructions from Cora. She had all the materials ready when they arrived, and registration opened smoothly right at noon. Cora assisted with the process until her speakers' meeting at 5pm. The workshop presenters, keynote speaker and conference workers all met to review the agenda. Last minute questions were answered and details were finalized. The meeting wrapped up at 6pm.

Cora spent the next few hours preparing the Crown Room for the kick-off session. She conducted a sound check, adjusted the participant tables, spoke with the vendors, and made sure that everything was in place. Cora was so wrapped up in the minutiae that she didn't notice Brent enter the room. He studied her closely. He had been inquiring about her throughout the day. The staff and speakers only had good things to say about her. She was organized, professional and in complete control. Why did this surprise him? When they were together, she appeared nervous and insecure at times. Cora fascinated Brent. After awhile, Brent slipped out the door. He didn't want her to know he was checking up on her.

By 7:00pm, Cora felt everything was done. She grabbed a quick dinner and went to her room. Her feet were killing her. She wasn't used to wearing heels all day. How did women do it? When she opened the door to her room, a large bouquet of flowers greeted her. She ran over and opened the card. It read, "I believe in you. Yours, Josh." Her heart melted and she grabbed her phone to call Josh. It was busy, so she left him a text instead.

'Thank you so much for the flowers. Your support means everything to me. Cora.'

They hadn't officially told each other the 3 word 'I love you' phrase yet. Cora didn't want to say it until she knew she meant it. Her conversation with Brent about love rang in her head throughout the day. She was pretty sure that she loved Josh, but shouldn't she know already? It wasn't a question she wanted to grapple with until work settled down. She was hoping her trip to Montana with Josh would provide her with the answers she was seeking.

Cora hadn't seen Brent the entire day. She thought he might come around and check in with her. He was impossible to read. One minute, he appeared concerned that she could handle things and the next, he left her on her own with full autonomy. Regardless, she would show him that she was more than capable. She needed a good reference if she intended to make it in this field.

Although it was still early in the evening, Cora decided against going out. She drew herself a bath and grabbed her romance novel. She closed her eyes and drifted off into relaxation. She about drowned herself when she heard the loud knocking on the door. There was no way she was going to answer it until she heard Brent's voice.

"Cora, I need to talk to you," Brent called out as he knocked loudly.

Cora wanted to simply hide under the bubbles, but she didn't. She grabbed a bathrobe and ran to the door. Her hair was still dripping when she opened it.

"Yes?" Cora said, a little out of breath.

"We have a problem," Brent said, as he entered her room.

"What's wrong?"

"I just received a call from Norm Biron and he is severely ill. He cannot present tomorrow," Brent said as he sat down in a chair. He was so concerned about the problem at hand that he hadn't noticed Cora's bathrobe when he walked in. After settling in his chair, he finally noticed and asked. "Did you want to change?"

"Give me a minute." Cora pulled out a pair of casual

clothes and went back into the bathroom. Her hair had little bubbles in it and the ends were all tangled together. She wrapped it up and clipped it on the top of her head. She put on a t-shirt and jeans. She had no make-up on. She was not at the top of her game physically, but most people weren't when they are forced out of a bath.

"Thank you for waiting," Cora said as she ran her hand through her wet hair. "I have a few ideas about another presenter. I was talking to Victor Mains today from Clean Energy. They are one of our new vendors at the conference. Anyway, the company just completed a research project on a new weatherization technique that uses environmentally friendly products, which in turn, cuts down on energy bills. It is even more cost-efficient than the current method. The research has just been published and is being well-received in the environmental community. We could ask Victor to present on how to conduct research on new innovative methods in addition to the outcome of his project. Or we could ask David Joyce to repeat his Thursday session tomorrow. This would offer participants the ability to make one of his sessions. There is a lot of interest in his materials."

Cora paced back and forth as she pitched her ideas as Brent listened intently.

"I know of Victor's work," said Brent. "Find him and ask him to present tomorrow. Let him know we will do whatever it takes to have him present."

"Will do," said Cora.

"Good job, Cora." Brent was pleased.

"Thank you," responded Cora. Finally, the man gave her a compliment.

"Nice flowers," Brent said, as he bent over to read the card from Josh. "I will see you tomorrow."

"Okay," she said

Why was Cora embarrassed that Brent saw the flowers from Josh? It wasn't like she was interested in Brent. He was obviously drop dead gorgeous; everyone would admit that fact. But his cold personality was impossible. Right when Cora felt the least bit comfortable around him, he pulled the carpet right out from underneath her. With Josh, she knew that he cared about her. He listened, for the most part. He agreed with her. He was stable. But why were these traits in Josh starting to annoy Cora?

It was so confusing. Brent came into Cora's life and all of the sudden, everything became a little fuzzy. Her work was more stressful, her relationship lost a little shine and she was starting to second-guess herself. Brent was simply wreaking havoc. Cora was not going to give him another victory. She pulled her thoughts together and got to work securing Victor Mains as a presenter.

After she got off the phone with Victor, Cora wasn't sure what she wanted to do. It was still early evening. Brent had triggered a spike in her adrenalin and she wasn't tired anymore. She was literally twiddling her thumbs when her phone buzzed. It was an alert that she received a text message. It was from Brent.

'Did you secure Victor?'

Honestly, this man was relentless. She did her duty and responded.

'Yes. Victor is confirmed.'

'Good. Come to the outside bar. I want you to meet someone.'

It was not even 9pm. Even though Cora was up for doing something, seeing Brent again was not what she had in mind. She could make up an excuse and see if that worked. Or she could tell him the truth that she didn't want to see him. After a few minutes she texted him back.

'I am talking to my boyfriend.'

That should surely sway Brent from bothering her. She deserved personal time. Right? Brent wasn't paying her right now.

'Come when you are done.' He messaged back.

It was not the response she expected. Did he ever respond how she expected? Maybe it wasn't all bad; she did want to get out a little. Due to her little boyfriend excuse, she had some time to get ready. She took time straightening her hair and putting on her makeup. It was an incredible place so Cora put on a casual yet classy outfit. She popped her heels back on and put on some dark lipstick. Cora took her time. She wanted Brent to wait and test his patience.

It was nearly an hour later when she made it down to the bar. For a Monday night, it was unexpected to see so many people out socializing. They all looked relaxed and happy. There was an uplifting contagious excitement in the air as the conversations grew louder. There were tables with views of the pool, garden and ocean. There were areas with couches surrounding small fire pits. Candles adorned the tables and flickered with each slight breeze. It was romantic. Cora wasn't sure why her heart dropped a little when she couldn't find Brent. Maybe she took a little too long. It was still a lovely evening and it felt good to be outside again in the salty ocean air where she could better hear the roar of the surf. She braced herself on the rail to view the ocean, stars and full moon. Her phone buzzed in her pocket.

'If you wanted to hide from me, you should have stayed in your room.'

Cora laughed as she read the message. She typed back. 'Where are you?'

'Right in front of you.'

Cora scanned the area again and sure enough, Brent was sitting on one of the couches with the fire pit. How did she miss him? She walked over to him and sat down. There were two half-empty wine glasses on the small table next to Brent. One had lipstick on it.

"Am I interrupting something?" Cora said, as she pointed to the glasses.

"No, but the person I wanted you to meet already left."

"Who was it?" Cora said with a slight tilt of her head.

"Someone very special to me."

"You aren't much for details," Cora said, as she twirled her finger through her hair.

"Quite the contrary. What do you want to know?" Cora wanted to know a lot of things, but a lot of questions she wasn't ready to ask.

"Was it Kate?"

"How did you guess? You can't imagine how much wine ghosts drink. And I thought you drank a lot."

"Funny," Cora said, even though she wasn't laughing.

"Since you offered a glass, I will take one."

"I didn't offer," Brent said, as he furrowed his eyebrows.

"You did when you made fun of my drinking."

Brent waved over the waiter and ordered Cora a Merlot.

"Do you ever wonder what I might like to drink?" Cora inquired with her arms folded across her chest.

"Did you want something else?"

"No, but it would be nice to be asked."

"Let me get this straight. I already know what you want, but you want me to ask you so you can tell me what I already know. Is this correct?" Brent said once again returning to his serious mode.

"When you put it like that, it sounds a little controlling."

"Just a little?" Brent said with his eyes of mischief.

Cora quickly changed the topic. "Are you close to your father?"

"We have gotten very close this past year. There have been a lot of changes in the company and in our family."

"Do you have any brothers and sisters?"

Brent was quiet for a moment and then said, "A brother."

They sat in silence for a few minutes. They did silence very well. Cora sat back and enjoyed feeling the breeze in her hair. When the music died down, she could hear the waves crashing. She warmed her hands by the fire and stared at Brent. He was incredibly handsome. He must have changed after he came to her room. He wore a polo shirt and a simple jacket. Brent's eyes locked with Cora's. He looked profoundly sad. Cora wanted to reach out to him, but she didn't know how. He was not a simple man. She didn't know what upset him, but she still leaned over and touched his hand. Much to her surprise, he let her. They sat for a few more minutes in silence. Cora kept her small hand upon his large hand. It was warm and smoother than she expected. Sharp jolts of energy shot through Cora.

"Life is unexpected, some of it good and some not so good."

"Has it been a difficult year for you, Brent?"

"Yes."

"I'm sorry to hear that."

"We have a big day tomorrow. I will walk you back to your room."

Brent left some money on the table and walked Cora to her room. There were no stops this time. Cora knew the routine and didn't balk when they walked up the three flights of stairs. Brent left after she opened her door. He said good night and vanished. Cora shut the door and sat on the bed. She felt like she might have just experienced a slight breakthrough with Brent. He showed her a side of himself that she did not anticipate. She wondered what caused him so much pain. In time, she hoped to find out.

More importantly, she wanted to explore her feelings about their interaction. She had touched other men before and not felt that connection. What did it mean? Cora finally admitted to herself that she was attracted to Brent. Cora did not lie to herself. It was one rule she didn't break. However, being attracted to Brent was complicated. He was hard on her and extremely difficult to figure out. She knew so little about him. Was he divorced? Did he have children? Was he seeing anyone? And even though she was attracted to him, he showed no signs of any interest in her. To top it off, he was so out of her league, not to mention her boss. She felt a little more settled about the issue after she spent the time to process it all. Just because she was attracted to the man, it didn't mean anything would come of it. She had a good, comfortable relationship with Josh and she was happy with that fact.

Cora woke up bright and early the next day. It was "show" time. The conference officially began at 9am, with breakfast at 8am. Cora was making her rounds at 7am to ensure that everything was perfect. She coordinated the location of the breakfast buffet tables and checked in with the hotel's conference manager. Registration was open and bustling with attendees. The keynote speaker was present. Everything was running smoothly. At precisely 9am, the conference began. Cora briefly caught eyes with Brent. She couldn't tell by his gaze if he was pleased with the event. She assumed he was, otherwise, he would have let her know. He was not the type of man to avoid expressing his displeasure.

As the conference host, Brent was the first to speak.

He thanked everyone for coming and spoke about the importance of their work in preserving the world for the next generation. Brent spoke about the importance of green jobs and how the field was growing every day. Cora was mesmerized. He spoke with poise and passion. He was a natural. Brent really engaged the audience and provided a fantastic opening to the conference.

The day flew by. Lunch was served at the tables. It was an exquisite three-course plated lunch. The meal began with wild mushroom bisque. The entrée was sliced beef tenderloin, mushroom fricassee, horseradish potato mousseline, English peas and carrots. Months ago, Cora insisted that Julie order the triple silk chocolate torte with black currant berries.

Unfortunately, Cora did not have time to sit and enjoy the lunch. The afternoon consisted of various workshops for the attendees. Cora wanted to make sure all of the audio visual equipment was in place, handouts ready and signage secured. Brent was a stickler for details and Cora didn't want one thing to be out of place.

After the workshops were in session, Cora turned her focus to the company dinner. It was set for 6pm in the Garden Room. It would be a small gathering of Locke Incorporated's board members. Once the dinner began, she would have some free time to herself. She wanted to do a few laps in the pool and sit in the spa. It would be nice to relax a little after all the day's events.

Focusing on her relaxing evening, Cora was able to push through the end of the day's agenda. There were a few issues which surfaced, but nothing that Cora couldn't handle and promptly resolve. So far, so good! At 5:30pm, Cora made her way from the Crown Room to the Garden Room. The room was empty when Cora arrived. It was completely transformed. The candles on the tables accented the soft lighting. Flowers were all over the room; hyacinths, gardenias, lilies, and gerbera daisies all splashed the room with bright color. The scents the flowers emitted were heavenly. Piano music entered from the door as Cora walked out to the garden patio. It was beyond romantic. The plush elegance blended well with the classy ambiance.

When Cora walked back into the room, she saw Brent. He had changed into a black double breasted sports coat with black slacks. He looked sharp and incredibly handsome. His jet black hair caught the reflection of the candlelight. He was something right out of a dream. Cora's mouth went dry. There was no longer any doubt; she was very attracted to him. She couldn't blame herself; any woman would melt in his presence.

In fact, she saw a lot of women watching him throughout the day. Their eyes trailed him after he walked past and lingered longer than mere curiosity. They were all probably wondering who he was and what it was like to catch his attention and hold it. Cora saw several women approach him and attempt to start a conversation. She tried not to laugh as he brushed them off. Little did they know, it had nothing to do with them, but Cora was beginning to recognize when Brent entered into his serious mode. Once he was in this serious mode, nothing could shake him out of it. He was focused like a laser on one thing and only one thing. Cora already knew what it felt like to experience this mode and she did not like it. The intensity was almost too much for her to handle. It made her nervous, and when she tried to help him, she found she was just in his way. Her best option was to remain quiet and disappear, if possible.

Disappearing from Brent was not easy. As Cora drifted off into her land of thoughts, Brent seemed to sense it. Cora wanted to check a few minor details regarding the dinner and then put her disappearing act into practice, but unfortunately, she was too late. Brent was by her side before she could dissipate like smoke.

"Are you going to change?"

"Yes. Right into my swimsuit," Cora said, confused as to why he was asking.

"I don't think that would be appropriate attire for a business dinner."

"Oh, I am not attending the dinner. It is only for board members," Cora reminded Brent.

"You should go and change. You have time before dinner is served. We can hold dinner if you are not back in time."

"Ok," Cora said, as she saw her relaxing evening disappear. It was not how she planned it.

"And Cora,"

"Yes," Cora said, as she turned back around.

"A dress would be more appropriate than a swimsuit," Brent said playfully.

Cora just walked out instead of replying with a snappy comment. She would show him. Cora might appear polite and docile, but she had a real spunk to her. Brent was starting to chew on her last nerve. She needed to start getting in the game and tonight she was going to begin.

Within less than 45 minutes, Cora returned to the dinner. It appeared that she was the last to arrive, which was perfect for her plan. She wanted to be noticed this time when she entered. She didn't need to worry about that. All of the men turned to look at her as she walked in. She wore a long floor-length black dress with a slit up the side that went almost to her thigh. She straightened her long black hair so it swayed very slightly as she walked. The front part of her hair framed her beautiful oval face. Her makeup was flawless and drew attention to her eyes. She had on a darker red lipstick to adhere to the social etiquette of an evening dinner. Her sleek black heels were almost the height of stilettos. Cora kept her jewelry simple yet elegant. She was stunning. Cora saw Brent take a double take when she walked over to him. It was precisely the reaction she wanted.

"Is my dress appropriate, Brent?" Cora asked, as she took the glass of wine he held out to her.

"Are you wearing a swimsuit under there? I wouldn't put it past you."

Cora couldn't help but laugh. "No, I am not."

"I saved a seat for you. Come sit down."

Cora thought she would be sitting near the back, but Brent led her to the head table and pulled out the chair beside his. They looked fabulous next to each other. The other seat near Brent was vacant, but not for long. A tall distinguished gentleman came over and gave Brent a very tight hug.

"Son, it is good to see you. We just got in two hours ago. You know how difficult it can be to get your mother out of the house. I've heard the conference is a huge success," the man said once their embrace ended. After he spoke, he noticed Cora. "And who is this raving beauty?"

"Cora, I would like you to meet my father, Robert Locke. Dad, this is Cora Jacobs."

Brent's dad lit up with excitement. "Corina Jacobs? Is your father Steven Jacobs?"

"Yes, he is. Do you know my father?"

"Know him? We went to USC together back in the day. We were in the same fraternity. I haven't seen him in years. How is he?"

"Great. He is enjoying his retirement more than my mom would like. She can't keep him off the golf course. They are living in Monterey now."

"I've met your sister, but I have been robbed of the pleasure of meeting you. What brings you here to The Del?"

"I am an intern with your company, Mr. Locke."

"That is fabulous. What are the odds? I take it you know my son, Brent. Is he treating you well?"

"Well enough," said Cora smiling as she looked over at Brent who looked a little flabbergasted. "Right, Brent?"

"Actually, Cora is doing more than interning. Julie couldn't oversee the conference this year, so Cora has stepped up and taken over," added Brent.

"So you are the mystery behind this year's success. I am not surprised. Your father has always spoken so highly of you. Now, come over here and sit next to me. I want to hear more about your father's golf game," Robert said, as he plucked Cora away from Brent and sat her next to him.

Robert was the warmth missing from Brent, Cora thought. He was completely open and the life of the party. Cora couldn't stop laughing. If he wasn't married, Cora would have been instantly in love. The family resemblance was undeniable. Robert had the same black hair sprinkled with a little gray. He dressed impeccably and carried himself with assured purpose.

He drew people in with his kindness and character. His charisma was magnetic.

By the end of the evening, Cora's cheeks and stomach were sore from all of the laughing. Robert told countless stories about Brent growing up. Stories about how Brent's intensity often got him into trouble. Robert also told her how Brent's sensitivity shaped him into a very compassionate man. Some of the things Robert shared really surprised Cora. She yearned to question Robert more, but knew that it wasn't appropriate. Dinner was wrapped up and dessert was already served. Cora was stuffed and completely satisfied.

"Having fun, Cora? You've stolen my dad from the rest of the group. I think he is smitten with you," Brent said.

Cora thought he was upset with her again. "I'm sorry, I can move to another table if you want."

"Are you kidding? I haven't seen my dad smile so much in quite a few months. It is nice to see him so happy. Thank you." Brent said, as he walked away and went on the garden patio. Cora followed him outside. The evening air was brisk and Cora did not have her coat. Brent took off his jacket and put it around her shoulders.

"Walk with me," Brent said. His sadness seemed to have returned. Was Cora misreading his mood? There were so many layers to Brent and Cora felt like she barely scratched the surface. She was beginning to realize that if he wanted to tell her something, he would. So she just walked next to him.

Even though it was a Tuesday evening, a lot of people were out and about. Small fires were scattered all over the beach. The moon was full and spilled a muted light all over the sand. Silhouettes danced with the incoming and receding water. Music from the outside bar of the hotel spread out in many directions. The fresh sea breeze was refreshing after being indoors all day. It had been a long day and Cora was starting to feel the impact.

"You still want that swim?" Brent inquired.

"I sure do."

"Go change and meet me back at the pool in ten minutes. I will be timing you. No lollygagging."

Cora practically ran back to her room. She wasn't sure why she listened to him. Half of her was infuriated and the other half intrigued. She should have felt guilty about not calling Josh, but the thought of Josh hadn't even crossed her mind. She quickly changed into her swimsuit and went down to the pool.

By the time she got there, Brent was already in the water doing laps. Cora took advantage of the dark night to stare at his body. His muscles rippled as his arms dug one right after the other through the water. His skin was dark mainly from his complexion and some from the sun. Brent's black hair was slicked back with wetness. Cora thought he looked even hotter than at dinner, if that was possible. As Cora watched Brent, he stopped at the side of the pool. He admired Cora in her black bikini. Her young body was tight and thin. She was beautiful, and even more so because she didn't know it.

"Come in," Brent said, desiring to see her body glisten in the moonlight.

Cora complied as she dove into the water.

"Wanna race?" Cora asked, as she took off.

Brent never turned down a good challenge and raced after her. She was more difficult to catch than he imagined. Little did Brent know, in college Cora was on the UC Berkeley swim team and still swam every week. Cora won the first lap and barely held on to the second.

"You must have cheated!" Brent said, as he playfully dunked Cora under the water.

"I don't think so. I beat you fair and square."

"Are you a mermaid? How did you do that? I just got whooped by a girl."

"Brent, you are not the only one full of surprises. Since I was the winner, you have to do as I say for the rest of the week," Cora demanded.

"Right."

"So you are in agreement?"

"I answer to no one," Brent said, as he splashed her with water.

"You are such a sore loser."

"How about a rematch?"

"We'll see. As the winner, there isn't much of an incentive for a rematch."

"Such a sharp little brainiac, aren't you?" Brent said with admiration.

"Oh, wait. Stop the presses. Are you giving me credit for something? I need to write this down."

"You are exaggerating again."

"Phew, that is more like it. I am more used to you correcting me. I was beginning to wonder if I can do anything right around you."

"You know that isn't true. Are you fishing for a compliment again?"

"Is there one available? You know, no one will keep track if you use one."

"Isn't that what you are doing right now? Keeping track? Putting words in my mouth? I am not a dog, Cora. I don't just do whatever you say."

"Hey, we are getting really far away from the fact that you were about to give me a compliment."

"I don't recall that," Brent bantered back.

"Of course you don't." Cora said, as she got out of the pool. The water was beginning to feel a little chilly, or maybe it was the conversation. She couldn't win with Brent. All she wanted was a little pat on the back. She worked her ass off for him and he said nothing. It was frustrating. As she began to walk away, Brent was quickly by her side. He grabbed her hand to stop her.

"I've upset you," Brent said, as he placed her hand in his.

"Now who's putting words in someone's mouth?"

"Fine. Speak for yourself. Why are you upset with me?"

"Just let it go," Cora said, now feeling rather silly for getting irritated. What was this man doing to her? She was usually the competent rational one. Here she was acting like a girl and she didn't like it.

"Corina." Cora stopped still.

"Only my grandmother and father call me by my given name. You aren't allowed," Cora responded with a moist fire in her eyes.

"You sure are feisty tonight. Let's go over to the spa and relax. You've had a really big day. You've been on your feet all day making sure everything was perfect. I was watching you. I have to say, I am impressed."

Finally! Was it really that difficult for him to give her the gratitude she desired? His dad barely knew her and he couldn't stop ranting and raving about her. While it was nice that Mr. Locke complimented her, she really wanted Brent to notice. What did he mean that he had been watching her? She barely saw him the whole day. She didn't really care at this point and was happy to hear him say something nice about her.

"Cora, what does your name mean? Wait, let me guess, spit, fire and vinegar?"

"Funny. Actually, there is a group of indigenous people in Mexico called Cora. They speak the Cora language. The Cora cultivate maize, beans and amaranth, and they raise cattle," Cora prattled off like she was reading out of a history book.

"Good to know. If I need a Cora interpreter, I know where to go."

Cora laughed at his silly response.

"Tell me more about your grandmother," Brent said once they were settled in the spa.

Cora was having a difficult time concentrating as she felt Brent's leg brush against hers in the spa. There were a few other people in the spa, so they needed to sit near each other. Cora was not complaining. It felt good to be near Brent with so few clothes on. Oh my goodness, did she really just think that?

"You check out every once in awhile, don't you?" Brent inquired.

"I was just thinking of my grandmother. You think I am a firecracker. She is just too much! I love to be with her. I feel so loved and special when I am in her presence. Unfortunately, I don't see her very often. The long flight is difficult for her to fly out here and my budget is pretty tight."

"Where does your grandmother live?"

"Back East. New York. She was born and raised there. She loves the hustle and bustle. I get my feisty side from her."

"Family is very important. Never lose sight of that fact," Brent said, once again looking rather distant and sad. Cora wasn't sure how to broach the subject so she tried to dance around it.

"You mentioned earlier that you are close to your father. Are you close to your mother and brother as well?"

"We've all had our share of differences, but when the important things have surfaced, we've supported one another."

"You don't reveal a lot of details, do you?"

"Not if I can help it. Everyone in my life is on a need

to know basis. If you don't need to know it, then I don't need to talk to you about it."

"That is one approach to life. I enjoy building relationships, and in order to do so, you need to trust people and share your thoughts and feelings."

"Is that how you approach your relationship with Bruce?"

"Who is Bruce?" Cora questioned, unsure of the name.

"Your boyfriend."

"His name is Josh. And I do share some of my thoughts and feelings with Josh," Cora replied curtly to Brent.

"Some? Not all? How do you decide what to share?"

"Why are you always turning things back on me? I asked you the question."

"Corina, there is no such thing as always and never."

Cora was beginning to wonder if she could do anything right around this man. Her face was getting flush and it wasn't from the hot water in the spa.

"Honestly, Brent. I am trying to get to know you, but you evade all of my questions."

"I don't evade all of your questions. You just don't like the answers I provide. Maybe you aren't asking the right questions."

"You provided answers?"

"You need to pay better attention, Cora."

Cora had enough and stood up to get out of the spa. At least when she was at work, she was paid to deal with Brent. But it was her own time now; she didn't have to stick around to be put down. Cora didn't care any more that he was insanely attractive. She had her limits too.

Before she made it out of the spa, Brent has his arms around her waist to stop her. They both felt the jolt of energy surge through them. Cora didn't back down as Brent stared right into her eyes. Brent took his right hand and brushed it lightly against her cheek. It was such a tender gesture that Cora was unsure what to do next. Brent's left hand remained on her waist and then moved to the small of her back. He gently pulled her toward him until their wet bodies touched. He ran his hand through her damp hair and trailed it down her back until his hands linked up. He pulled her even closer; so close that she could feel his rock hard bulge grow even harder. The reality of their sexual tension should have caused fear or alarm in Cora, but it only spurred her on. She wanted more. She yearned for his lips to be on hers, but he didn't make another move. Their eyes were still locked together. They were teetering on the edge of something, but neither was willing to make the next move.

Brent leaned over and whispered in Cora's ear, "Cora, I

am sorry."

Then he kissed her on the forehead and stepped out of the spa. He wrapped a towel around his waist and took Cora's hand to lead her out of the spa. He wrapped a towel around her waist, took another towel and began to dry her hair. Unbelievable! He had just treated her so kindly. Cora was in shock. Her words would not form, so she just observed this rare glimpse at Brent's sensitive side.

"I enjoy our time together, Cora. As you know, I am an independent man. I don't play by everyone else's rules. It may seem like I am being hard on you, but I won't sugarcoat the truth. I can tell that you want to know more about me and I have averted revealing much. When I am with you, I find I want to be more expressive. There are some things that are important that you should know about me before this goes any further. You have asked about the children in my life, I am their…"

"Brent! Cora! I've been looking for you everywhere," Brent's father said as he rushed over to them.

Cora was not happy to see him. Brent was finally beginning to open up to her and now they were interrupted. She needed to find a way to get rid of Robert quickly.

"Brent, your mother is back at the villa and she insists on seeing you tonight. I promised her that I would find you. I've been calling your cell phone, but you didn't answer. Would you please go see her so she will stop nagging me?"

Brent didn't seem like he wanted to go, but he said to his father, "Of course. After I make sure Cora gets safely back to her room, I will visit mother."

"I will walk Cora to her room so you can go visit your mother. It would be my pleasure to escort such a beauty safely back to her room. You have had her long enough, Brent," Robert said with a little sparkle in his eye. He didn't seem to mind the duty.

"Cora, don't let my father keep you up. You have a full day of work tomorrow."

"Yes, Boss," Cora said as she saluted Brent as he walked away.

Cora had a tough time being upset with Robert. He was charming and a gentleman that knew what the ladies liked to hear. Cora quickly changed in the pool's locker room. She suddenly felt funny being half-naked in front of Brent's dad, especially after feeling Brent's member against her body just moments before. When Cora emerged from the locker room, Robert locked his arm into Cora's.

"Your escort is at your service. Shall we stop off at the bar for a little refreshment, first?"

"As you wish, Robert." Cora could not turn him down.

She had a wonderful time with Robert. They picked up right where they left off at dinner. There was only one awkward moment when Robert asked if she was seeing anyone. Cora felt reluctant to tell him about Josh. She still didn't know if Brent was available. Robert didn't have much to say when Cora told him that she had a boyfriend. Robert just said that Josh was a very lucky man.

Chapter 6

Cora didn't see much of Brent at the Conference on Wednesday. It wasn't until late afternoon on Thursday that they ran into each other.

"I would like to review Friday's agenda with you tonight. I will pick you up at your room at 6:30pm," Brent said in passing.

Cora was starting to accept Brent's abrupt nature. She was past trying to fight it and started to go with it instead. She made sure she was ready in her room at 6:15pm. Brent was punctual and did not like to be kept waiting and Cora felt the same way about time.

"Let's take a walk on the beach and then go to dinner," Brent said a he headed toward the stairs.

They walked down to the beach and reviewed Friday's agenda. It was going to be the final day of the conference. The luau would occur on Friday night. It would be Cora's last official business duty for the week. Julie had scheduled an extra day at The Del to debrief and relax. Since Julie wasn't there, Cora would have the entire day to herself. She had mixed emotions about it all. She was relieved that the stress would be over soon, but she had enjoyed the challenge. Brent seemed content with her responses to his numerous final day agenda logistical questions. He actually gave Cora a semi-compliment, which was unusual for him.

While they were walking back along the beach toward The Del, a little blond girl ran over to Brent and threw her arms around his legs. She squealed with joy as Brent threw her up in the air. Cora had never seen Brent so happy. He was a completely different person. His serious business mode was instantly replaced with a sensitive, loving and joyful side. An older boy building a sandcastle pulled Brent over to view his masterpiece. The boy was about four or five, with jet black hair like Brent. The resemblance to Brent was unmistakable. A distinguished woman in about her early 60's rose from a beach chair and walked over to Brent.

The children ran over to her and cried out, "Grandma, Grandma! Look who we found!"

There was no doubt that the woman was Brent's mother. She had the same penetrating stare as Brent as she looked Cora up and down. Cora felt the chill right down to her bones. His mother seemed very displeased to see her; she was not a woman to upset.

"Mother, this is Cora Jacobs, one of our company interns. Cora, this is my mother, Leslie," Brent said as he introduced Cora.

"I've heard about you Cora," she bluntly and harshly responded, "Robert cannot stop talking about Steven's daughter." Brent's mother literally turned her back on

Cora as she obviously only wanted to speak to Brent.

"Brent, darling," his mother said in a sweet voice, "You're coming out to dinner with us, right? The children have been asking about you all day."

Cora could see where Brent got his abrupt harsh nature. "Mother, I already have dinner plans with Cora," Brent replied.

"Oh, darling, who is more important than the children? They miss you and have barely seen you all week. I am sure Cora understands that family is more important than business. Right, Cora?"

Cora felt trapped. She took the safest ground she could find.

"It is entirely up to Brent," Cora said quietly and respectfully.

"Oh good, then it is settled. Brent, you go and give the children a bath. They can't go out with sand in their hair. Cora, give your father our best. Goodbye."

Brent's mother had the children packed up in record time and smoothly shuffled Brent away. Brent didn't appear to notice Leslie's cold attitude toward Cora. He didn't even apologize for skipping dinner. Not that she would have gone, but it wouldn't have hurt for him to invite her to go with his family. He glanced over her shoulder and gave Cora a brilliant smile as he walked away with both children in his arms. It was very clear that Brent's mother did not want Cora anywhere near

Brent. Was she protecting Brent's wife or girlfriend? The children were definitely Brent's. It was undeniable.

She was pretty disappointed as she went back to her room. Besides Brent, she didn't know anyone well enough to go out to dinner with them. It didn't really matter, she had lost her appetite. She should have been excited to have time to herself, but she could no longer deny the feelings which grew stronger each day she spent with Brent. It was crazy; she did not understand it, but he stirred something in her that she never felt before. Her temper got a workout around him, but she also felt empowered, attractive, competent and at her best this week. Brent was a real man. It was amazing to be around someone that knew how to take charge and make a decision. They were obviously attracted to each other, but now that she met his children, it was obvious why he was holding back. The only question left unanswered was, where was their mother?

Cora spent the evening in her hotel room. She half expected Brent to knock on her door, but it didn't happen. She called Josh and talked to him for a bit about nothing important. He was very excited about their upcoming trip. Cora didn't share the same enthusiasm. She didn't want to go in the first place, and after such a hectic week, she would have preferred going to a remote island in the middle of nowhere. At least the middle of nowhere, part of her fantasy would happen in Montana. Cora tried to enjoy her evening, but she was pretty low. She flipped through the channels on TV, and after finding nothing, she went to sleep. Even though Brent was never hers, she felt like he had just slipped through her fingers.

Friday was a complete blur. The last day of the conference was jam-packed with workshops, main sessions and demonstrations. Cora split her time between the conference and preparing for the luau. She was extra diligent and threw herself into her work. She purposefully avoided any contact with Brent. If she saw him approaching, she quickly turned and went the other way. She knew he would want to talk about his children and their mother. Cora wasn't ready for the truth. She wanted to hold on a little longer to her unrealistic fantasy. Her time with Brent at The Del had been magical. It was all about ready to come to a close. It was 5pm; the conference was officially over and deemed a huge success.

Cora went back to her room to change for the luau. She wore a long white cotton dress with flowers on it. She placed a beautiful red flower in her hair and slipped on some sandals so she could navigate the sand without embarrassing herself. She wore her grandmother's silver bracelet and silver hoop earrings. Cora gazed at herself in the mirror. She looked smoking hot and she knew it. She accented her lips with a deep red lipstick and went down to the party.

The luau was in full swing upon her arrival. The Del staff went all out. Tiki torches lined the entire perimeter of the event. Two huge white tents held the majority of the guests. Spouses and children of the attendees were invited. Cora projected that over 700 would attend. Tropical flowers hung from every available pole. Elegant flower arrangements sat on top of glass pillars on each table. There were too many candles lit up everywhere to count them all. A wooden dance floor was set up and a band was playing background music. Chicken, rice, salmon, sweet potatoes, mahi-mahi, poke and other traditional foods were abundant. For an added touch, each guest received a lei as they provided their entry ticket. Cora couldn't wait to see how the pigs cooked in the ground would taste. She watched the preparations and was excited to see the results. Cora knew The Del staff by name due to her countless trips between the conference and the luau preparations. They greeted her warmly and she thanked them for all of their hard work. It was better than Cora imagined. She enjoyed hearing how impressed the guests were as they took it all in. Cora hoped that Brent would be proud of her.

Cora walked down to the water and gazed back at The Del. Within the last week, she grew even more attached to its grandeur. The spirit of The Del was so strong. So many once stood and viewed its splendor just as Cora was doing. A slight breeze tousled Cora's hair. She could sense a presence and she wondered if Kate was near. Gloom overcame Cora's heart for a brief moment as Cora pondered how Kate must have felt when her lover never showed up to claim her. When Cora first heard Kate's story, she felt compassion for her, but also scoffed at all the hoopla created around the story. However, as she stared back at The Del, she fully comprehended Kate's despair. To be in love and to be hurt so deeply by a man; no woman wanted that to happen to her. Cora wondered if she would ever feel that passionate and loving towards a man. Her heart was so confused. She still didn't know what it meant to be in love. As silly as it sounded, she wished she could talk to Kate. Cora wanted to know what it felt like to love someone so deeply that you would give your life away because you couldn't be with them.

Cora jumped when she felt a hand on her arm.

"Where are you Cora? I've been watching you and you seem so far away. Take me there," Brent said as he gazed into her eyes.

"I was just thinking about Kate again. Brent, why does her spirit stay here? Was her heart so broken that she still refuses to let go? Which would have been worse for her, being abandoned by her husband or him taking her life? There are far more questions than answers."

"That is life, Cora. There are many things that happen which don't make sense at the time and some things seem to never make sense."

"I thought there was no such thing as 'never'," Cora said, proud to have caught Brent at breaking one of his own rules.

"Let me clarify. The word 'never' is merely one extreme viewpoint. It is set. Final. There is no wiggle room in the word 'never'. I said sometimes it feels like things will never make sense. We can get so caught up in our emotions that we lose the ability to focus on the truth. "

"I hadn't looked at it that way," Cora said quietly.

"Perhaps someday we will understand things like why someone dies what we call a premature death. I don't know," Brent said as he turned to face the ocean.

He took a cigar from his shirt pocket and lit it. He was a man. She had known him for months now and was learning new things about him every day. From the first day she met him, she knew he was a true man by the way he carried himself with a self-confidence and purpose. His intense gaze, whether focused on something or simply lost in his own thoughts, could penetrate right through you. Everything he did appeared driven by some unseen force from within. He was independent from even the concept of dependence. He was a leader you just wanted to follow. There was no choice in the matter; not that he would force you to follow him. You just knew he would take you to exactly where you needed to go. He was safe, yet alluringly dangerous. He was everything she had ever wanted and more.

Cora felt perfectly at peace. Since she wasn't sure how long it would last, it was even more important for her to capture every single minute in her heart. Her week at The Del was the most enchanting and romantic she had ever experienced. Cora stared at The Del and let it all soak in. The hotel was simply magnificent. It stood in perfect majesty and glory like a crown jewel. The flags on top of the castle-like-peaks flapped in the wind. Several lights in windows reminded her that life did exist and she was not dreaming. It was all so perfect.

The red glow of the cigar brought Cora back to the moment at hand. Brent was now lost in his own world.

They spent a tremendous amount of their time together in silence. It seemed to work for them both. Unfortunately, the silence was quickly interrupted by Brent's annoying mother.

"Darling, there you are. I have been looking for you. Why do you keep disappearing? Grace needs you. She is over by the dance floor. She needs your help with one of the children," Brent's mother, Leslie, said as she glared at Cora.

"Thanks, mother. I will go find Grace. Cora, I will have to catch up to you later. I want to try out the dance floor," Brent said as he gave her a little wink.

Cora was left alone with The Viper and needed a rapid escape. A dance with Brent sounded fun, if she managed to get away from his mother. She wasn't sure who Grace was, but it didn't take her long to find out. Cora saw Brent approach a gorgeous tall, blond woman. She wore a classy black cocktail dress with a long strand of pearls wrapped delicately around her neck. Her hair was short and chic. Her shoes had to be Prada; they were to die for. As Brent approached her, she met him with a warm hug and brief kiss on the lips. Brent slipped an arm around her waist and then picked up the little blond toddler Cora had seen on the beach.

"They are the perfect family," Leslie said with proud delight.

"Family?"

"Grace and Brent. Even though she is my daughter-in-law, Grace is everything I have ever wanted in a daughter. I couldn't be happier. Grace comes from a long line of established family lineage. She knows the importance of family. She is the best mother. Have you had the pleasure of meeting her?"

"No," Cora said, fighting back tears.

"I'm surprised that you haven't had dinner with them. Grace is an incredible cook. My husband mentioned you have a boyfriend. The four of you have to get together sometime. I'll be sure to mention it to Grace. Aren't you just an intern?"

"Yes," Cora said quietly.

"Grace has an MBA and experience in the private and public sectors. She's always willing to help the less fortunate and people as they are starting out. People like you." Leslie seemed to enjoy demeaning and minimizing Cora. She was a cold woman. "You should really start looking into landing your first real job. You're already getting a little old to be an intern. Plus, an internship is not real employment."

Cora hadn't even thought about her next steps after the internship. She was hoping to be picked up by Locke Incorporated. She had been so lost in her attraction for Brent that she wasn't thinking about her career. Now she was stuck listening to his mother prattle on and on about how wonderful Grace was, and how happy she made Brent. After listening for a few minutes, Cora couldn't take anymore. Tears began to collect in Cora's eyes. The last thing she wanted was for The Viper to see her cry.

Cora gathered all of the strength within her and said, "Please excuse me, I need to go check in with the event staff. I have got to go. Goodbye, Mrs. Locke."

Cora held her head high as she walked off. She checked in with the event staff to let them know she would be in her room, if needed. Cora made sure to avoid any possible contact with Brent. She walked back to her room and shut the door. It was then that the tears fell. She didn't realize how deep her feelings ran for Brent. She felt set up and so stupid to think that someone like Brent could be romantically interested in her.

No wonder he was so resistant to move things forward the other night. He had a wife and two beautiful children. She couldn't compete, and it wasn't her style to go after a married man. She was convinced that she had made a fool of herself around him. The things she shared with him, her boss... her married boss. How he toyed with her! Why didn't he just tell her? Of course, she never outright asked him and he wasn't the type to supply information. He probably assumed Julie had told her. Maybe he thought that Cora was the type that went after married men.

Cora's head was spinning. She was going to be sick. She rushed to the window and pushed it open. The fresh breeze felt good on her face. She could hear the faint sound of the music from the luau. Her tears continued to fall. The breeze would dry one, but another rushed to take its place.

Cora turned away from the window and realized her room was dark. In her rush to hide from Brent and his mother, she forgot to turn on the light in her room. The darkness fit her mood. Plus, if anyone was looking for her, they would see the light was off and assume she was asleep or not in her room.

Cora sat down by the bed and kicked off her shoes. In her earlier haste to leave the luau, she ripped her dress on one of the chairs and her make-up was now smeared all down her face. Not only did she look like a clown, but she felt like one. The flower in her hair had already fallen on the floor and was crushed in pieces. Looking into her mirror with tears in her eyes she was startled by the vibration from her cell phone announcing a text message. It must be Josh, she thought, but as she peered over at the beginning of her text message she read:

'Ready to dance?'

Cora threw her phone across the room. As much as she wanted to, she was not going to respond to him. She was done playing games. There would be no more dinners or any dancing. She would be nobody's fool. Cora didn't know what his intentions were, but it no longer mattered. Cora was through with Brent Locke.

About a half hour later, Brent knocked on Cora's door. "Cora? Are you in there? The event staff said you would be in your room."

Cora remained still and did not answer.

A moment later her cell phone vibrated. Thank goodness she left the ringer off. It was Brent. She did not answer. After a few minutes, Brent left the hallway. Cora lay down on her bed and sobbed. When did her heart get so taken by this man? Cora eventually fell asleep for several hours.

As she lay on the bed, Cora felt a coolness descend upon her whole being. A dull green light filled every inch of the room. The curtains began to move by the window. In the shadows, Cora saw the silhouette of a woman. It had to be Kate. Cora was not afraid. She felt a comfortable connection with her presence.

"Kate, I know you are here."

Then a woman's shadow moved toward Cora and reached out to her. The woman wore a long floor-length dress and her long black hair was pulled back by a ribbon. Her face was emotionless. It was like Cora was looking at a 3-D hologram. There was no doubt in Cora's mind she was looking right into the eyes of Kate Morgan. She felt an ever so slight yet powerful touch in her hair and a faint whisper–like moan. Cora thought about turning on the light to get a better look at Kate, but she didn't dare. She didn't want to frighten her away. Kate did not speak, so Cora tried to talk to her.

"Kate, I wish you could talk to me. I have so many questions for you."

Cora was unsure if she should ask Kate about how her death occurred. She had no experience with the paranormal and was completely out of her element. For a few minutes, they simply stared at one another. It was oddly comforting. Suddenly, Kate walked away from the bed and moved toward the door. She stopped at the door and looked back at Cora. Cora quickly put on some sandals and opened the door. Kate walked ahead of her and down the hallway. Kate paused out front of her room but kept walking. It must have been about 2am in the morning. There were no guests in the hallway, which was a relief to Cora. While there was a part of her that wanted someone else to witness Kate, she also didn't want Kate to disappear. Kate continued to walk down the hallway and stopped once they reached a small stairwell. She glanced back at Cora to see if she was following. Kate walked down the stairs until they were outside. It had cooled off considerably since Cora was at the luau. Without any concerns, Cora continued to follow behind Kate.

Kate stopped on the hotel stairs that led guests down to the beach. It was the same area Brent had told Cora that Kate had died. The light above the stairs flickered as Kate walked under it. All of the sudden, the bulb popped and the light went out. Kate began to move her mouth, but no words came out. Cora could tell she was trying to communicate with her.

"I heard this is where you died." Kate just stared at Cora. "Did you kill yourself?" Kate kept staring. "Did someone murder you?"

Kate slowly closed her eyes and then reopened them; as

if acknowledging that Cora was correct. Kate then turned from Cora and walked toward the water. As she walked towards the ocean, her image completely dissipated into the air.

Cora was shaken. It was an astonishing experience. It was so unbelievable that she wasn't sure she believed it herself. Cora sat down on the stairs so she could soak it all in. Why did Kate choose to appear to her that very night? Could she sense Cora's broken heart? And why did she want Cora to come down to where she died? Was she trying to tell someone about her death? Is that why she still haunted The Del? Once again, Cora had so many questions with no answers.

Was Cora's destiny fated to follow Kate's broken heart? Cora was physically and emotionally exhausted. She had experienced a lot of highs and some serious lows during the past week. She fell in love, only to be bitterly disappointed. She seemingly had more in common with Kate than she wanted to admit. Cora returned to her room in a serene and confident state and quickly entered a deep and peaceful sleep that lasted until the morning. She awoke that Saturday morning questioning whether last night was a dream; nevertheless, something profound had occurred and it was pushing her to really look at her life. She realized she had not yet found her destiny and a life that was truly worth living.

It was time for Cora to make a choice. She could either enjoy her sadness or do something about it. Brent was unavailable and Cora had a good relationship with Josh. It was not even a choice. She had to break off any personal relationship with Brent in order to preserve what was left of her heart. It wouldn't be that difficult since Brent was rarely at the office. Plus, once Cora put her mind to something, nothing deterred her.

Chapter 7

It was early Saturday morning when Cora decided it was time to leave. Although Cora was scheduled for an extra day at The Del, she wanted to get back home. She didn't want to risk seeing Brent or any of his family. She was completely done with all of the Lockes. It was raining, which fit Cora's depressed mood perfectly.

The cab arrived on time and Cora was able to avoid seeing anyone she knew. As the cab drove away, Cora looked back one more time at The Del. She swore she saw the curtains in her room move, but wasn't quite sure.

Regardless of the turn of events, Cora thoroughly enjoyed her time at The Del. She would never forget what it had given her and also what it so quickly took away. Her father had taught her that life was meant to be lived at its fullest. He strongly believed one can't judge the fairness of one's life in the short term – as circumstances and conditions are forever changing. He believed that we are in control to create a great life, fully expressing our deepest life purpose. And that we also can choose to live the life of a victim, in which we pretend that we are responsible for creating our sadness by focusing on negative thoughts and actions. She was doing her best at this time to lean into this encouragement to live with an open and honest heart. Looking back, Cora really believed that her connection with Brent had actually brought out the best in both of them. She had felt alive and it was a time in her life that she would seal in her heart forever.

Cora's phone rang twice that day. The first call was from Josh. He was happy that she was returning early. He promised to pick her up from the airport. He couldn't wait to hear all about her week. She had been so busy that she didn't have the chance to talk to Josh much during the week. Hearing his voice brought Cora a little comfort. They would be leaving for Montana on Monday, which was now more appealing to Cora. She was ready to be out of California for a little while. She wanted to refocus on her relationship with Josh and start planning her future.

The second call was from Brent. She didn't answer it. He left her a voicemail, but she deleted it before she listened to it. She didn't care what he had to say. She was on vacation and didn't owe him anything. He was a married man and completely off limits.

The flight to Columbia Falls with Josh was ordinary. Cora had never been to Montana. Country life did not appeal to her, but she was willing to spend a week there. It was a small price to pay to be with Josh. He was beyond excited. It had been almost a year since Josh had been home and he couldn't wait to see everyone. The only family member Cora had met was

Josh's younger sister. Cora was feeling a little gun-shy to meet his parents, still recovering from the treatment she got from Brent's mother. She hoped they liked her and she hoped she could at least tolerate them.

Columbia Falls was the largest town outside of Glacier National Park. The border with Canada was about an hour to the north. Josh grew up on a cattle ranch a few miles out of town. He was the third generation of his family to live in Montana. Cora wasn't sure why, but this made her uncomfortable. Her family did not have any roots in a set place, so perhaps it was just an unrealistic fear of the unknown.

When the plane landed, Josh practically hopped out of the plane.

"The snow will fly anytime now. Maybe if we are lucky, it will begin while we are here. Cora! Look! The fall leaves are still on the trees."

Cora was spellbound. She had never seen such picturesque mountains before. The green pines dominated the landscape, yet patches of yellow birches and red liquid ambers popped up, dispersed in the sea of green. White puffy clouds sat high up in the sky. It was a sharp contrast to the bright blue sky. All the colors swam around in her head. It was incredible.

"Josh, you didn't tell me how beautiful it is here."

"Sweetheart, I have told you countless times. I don't think you wanted to believe it."

Cora laughed. She was a city girl at heart. "You're right. I believe you now."

"I see my mom and dad. It looks like they brought Grandma too!" Josh rushed into the arms of a short, round older woman. Her gray-white hair was wrapped in a bun on the top of her head.

"Grandma, you look just as beautiful as the last time I saw you."

"Joshua, you are too good to me," his grandma said as she blushed.

"Grandma, this is Cora."

"I am very pleased to meet you," Cora said genuinely.

"Come here, sweetheart and give Grandma a hug. I have heard so much about you from my Joshua. You are such a beautiful woman, just as he described."
Cora was now the one blushing. "Thank you. That is very kind of you."

Josh pulled Cora over to his mom and dad. They were exactly as Cora imagined: the classic rancher and his wife. Josh's mom wore a plaid flannel shirt and his dad had on overalls.

"Mom, Dad, I'd like to introduce you to Cora."

Josh's mom pulled her into an embrace. She said, "Thank you so much for coming to spend Thanksgiving with us. We have missed our son. He said you convinced him to come. It means the world to me. Someday when you are a mother, you will understand what it means to spend time with your children."

Josh's dad shook Cora's hand and mumbled a hello. He appeared pretty shy, but Cora could see a slight tear in his eye when Josh hugged him.

"Cora, do you know how to ride?" Josh's mom said as they headed toward baggage claim.

"No. I haven't been on a horse, but I am willing to learn."

"That's the spirit! Josh was practically born on a horse. He is the best teacher. You'll be a pro in no time. Josh has quite the seat."

"Seat?" Cora asked, confused by the terminology.

Josh's mom laughed, "I'm sorry. Seat is a riding term which refers to how someone sits on a horse."

"Oh, ok." Cora had more to learn than she realized. At least Josh's mom wasn't condescending. She was very kind and helpful. It was a refreshing change from Brent's mother.

The ride to the family ranch was pleasant. Josh was involved in a passionate conversation with his mom and grandma. Josh's dad was stoic as he drove the truck home. Cora wasn't sure if she had ever ridden in such a large truck. Josh referred to it as a 6-pack diesel dually. Cora had no idea what he was talking about, so she smiled and nodded.

The scenery out the window caught Cora's attention. They passed several streams and a large bustling river. In the middle of Columbia Falls was a large metal bridge, which spanned across the bubbling water below. The sun was edging down behind the mountains. The deep orange and red colors reflected off the water and bounced up to the trees. It was so peaceful, yet even among Josh's family, Cora felt a little lonely. Just two days ago, she was at the ocean, caught up in the allure of Brent Locke. Now she was physically miles away, yet her heart was still right there at The Del. Cora was hoping that eventually her heart would come to its senses and realize that it belonged with Josh. Her head knew it, but her heart was foolishly rebellious. Thank goodness Cora's head ruled her life. Always. Maybe always and never were pretty firm as Brent had told her. Cora didn't actually see any wiggle room at all in those words. Why did Brent have to be so right?

Josh did not notice Cora's distance. He was too wrapped up in his conversation to notice much of anything else. Cora was fine with it. She wanted a little time to lick her wounds and heal. Montana would provide her the opportunity for just that.

The family ranch was about 20 minutes outside of Columbia Falls. Cora was excited to learn that the entire ranch covered over a thousand acres. Cora had a difficult time wrapping her mind around the size. She grew up in the classic suburbs where property was measured more in square feet and partial acres. She couldn't imagine why anyone needed so much land. What did you do with it all? Did cows really need that much space? Cora's first lesson with the cows began as they drove up to the ranch gate. A horrendous smell entered the truck when Josh's dad opened the gate. Cora's stomach churned.

Josh leaned over and whispered, "You'll get used to the smell. After awhile, you won't even notice it."

Cora had a difficult time imagining that would ever happen and gave Josh a weak smile. Cows were everywhere. Both sides of the driveway were lined with cows. Josh shed some light on the situation.

"We bring the cattle down from the upper ridge before the snow flies. We keep them close to the covered areas for the winter."

"Oh," Cora said as she stared at the endless sea of cows.

When the truck stopped, Josh climbed out and dragged Cora by the hand to the horse barn.

"Come on, I'll give you the full tour."

Cora tried to be interested, but after hearing the breeding, make and model of the 20th horse, Cora was downright bored. She was starting to wonder how she was going to survive a week in the country. After the never-ending tour was over, Cora pumped Josh for some information about the activities of the week.

"What is the plan for the week?" Cora asked.

"Plan? Well, we will celebrate Thanksgiving on Thursday with a family dinner."

"And...?" Cora said, knowing there was more.

"Actually, I hadn't planned too much out. My dad needs some help on the back 40, so we can ride out there tomorrow if you'd like."

"Oh, ok," Cora was actually not that serious about learning to ride a horse, but she did tell his mom that she would learn.

"Is there something you wanted to do? You could help my mom prep the Thanksgiving meal on Wednesday. She is expecting about 20 guests so I am sure she would appreciate the help."

"Oh, ok." Cora wasn't the best in the kitchen, but she was good at washing dishes.

"I pretty much thought we would just hang out around the ranch this week. Is that alright?" Josh asked.

"I wanted to see a little more of the area. Glacier National Park is close. I was interested in checking that out."

"Of course. I am sure my mom would lend you her car for the day," Josh said happy to help.

Cora was a little surprised that Josh didn't offer to go

with her, as she thought this was their vacation. He seemed focused on the ranch now that they were on his turf. Maybe she was being overly sensitive. She could plan out the day and then convince him to go along. She would just have to bat her eyes a little.

"Let's go see what is for dinner," Josh said as they walked back toward the house.

Their family dinner was very nice. Josh's family was very talkative; even his dad made a comment or two. They were visibly happy to have Josh back home. Josh was acting much different than the Josh Cora was used to being around in California. He was extremely focused on getting up to speed on the cattle business and hearing all the neighborhood gossip. He came across manlier when he talked business, and it turned Cora on. When Josh took Cora to his sister's room, she expressed to him how hot he sounded when he talked business.

"This little cowgirl is ready for some wrangling. Why don't we try and rustle something up?" Cora said as she lunged at Josh's pants.

Josh pulled back with a surprised look on his face. "We can't do this here. My grandma could walk in." Cora was not deterred.

"Then lock the door," Cora said as she rubbed her hand across the bulge in his pants.

"Cora. We are staying in my parents' home in separate rooms out of respect for my grandmother. This is not right," Josh said scolding her.

Cora was disappointed and pulled her hands away. "Oh, ok. I guess I will see you in the morning."

"We have a big day tomorrow; get some rest," Josh said as he kissed her cheek.

"Good night." Cora was unsure if he heard her.

Cora spent some time rooting through her suitcase. Then she spent about an hour attempting to find the exact spot to stand in order to check her email on her phone. Right when she got a bar of service, it would go out again. She finally discovered if she stood on a chair close to the window, she got reception. Her email was pretty full. She hadn't checked it while at The Del. There was a lot of spam, a message from her roommate, two messages from Julie and one email address she didn't recognize. The subject line said 'departure' and was sent on Sunday. The message read:

Corina,

I attempted to find you for the dance you promised me. I also looked for you on Saturday, as my father and I wanted to take you out to dinner to thank you for your outstanding job on the conference. We were both impressed with your level of professionalism, customer service and dedication for such a high level of responsibility. You were superb!

I was surprised to hear from the hotel staff that you checked out a day early. I hope it was nothing urgent that took you from your well deserved day of relaxation at The Del.

Since I could not thank you in person, I have placed something on your desk. Enjoy your well-earned vacation.

Thanks again!
Brent

Cora wasn't sure what to make of Brent's email. What did he place on her desk? He was a little confused about her promising him a dance. He was the one insisting that they dance. She couldn't stay completely mad at him. He gave her such a sincere compliment. He even sounded like he was proud of her. She had worked so hard all week for that acknowledgement. Now that it had finally arrived in an email, she was confused by her feelings and emotions. Cora's fascination with Brent returned.

Every woman would want a man like Brent to play some role in her life. Cora had already learned a lot from him. It wasn't like he made a pass at her or said something inappropriate. How could she be angry with him due to her own feelings? It was unfair of her. Interacting with Brent caused Cora to think a lot more and she wasn't used to it. However, some introspection was good in order to acknowledge her weaknesses and her strengths. It was probably what made her feel so alive and at her best.

Cora sat in bed for a while thinking about Brent's email. She thought about discussing it with Josh, but she wasn't sure how he would respond. Cora and Josh weren't that open in their communication. They rarely discussed much about their work and Josh wasn't into sharing his feelings. Then again, she didn't know too many men that believed in being fully expressed. Most men seemed to gunny sack their real thoughts and feelings in their relationships.

When Cora went down the hallway to brush her teeth, she heard Josh talking to his dad about the cattle and branding season. At first it was a turn on, but now Cora was tiring of hearing about the business. Instead of joining him, she went back to her room and responded to Brent's email:

Brent,

Thank you for the kind words. I am glad Locke Incorporated was pleased with my work performance. I feel honored that I have had the opportunity to be an intern with your company.

Cora

Her written response was very professional and more formal than Brent's. She wanted to ensure that her interactions with him focused 100% on her career. She needed to be cautious of chain emails that could be misinterpreted, or worse, end up in the hands of others. Grace seemed to be an understanding woman. She likely wouldn't be against Brent communicating and mentoring Cora.

The next day started far earlier than Cora wanted. Josh

was in her room at 5:00am, dressed and ready to roll. Cora dragged herself out of bed and threw on some clothes. Josh's mom had breakfast ready and Cora poured herself a large cup of black coffee.

"I put some riding boots out for you, Cora. They belong to Josh's sister. If they are a little big, you can double up your socks," Josh's mom said as she handed Cora a jug of cream.

"Fresh cream is one benefit of living on a ranch," Josh said proudly.

"Is this a dairy farm?" Cora asked.

Josh burst out laughing. "Sweetheart, we raise our cattle for the slaughterhouse. Our neighbors bring us the fresh cream in exchange for meat."

Cora wasn't sure why her question was so funny to Josh. She was starting to wonder about his sense of humor.

"Josh tells me you were just in San Diego. Was it nice? I heard the weather is warm all year-round. Is that true or a wild rumor?" Josh's mom pleasantly interjected, probably trying to ease the slight tension in the room.

"The weather was incredible. Our conference was at a fabulous historic hotel. I've never experienced anything like it. Have you heard of the Hotel del Coronado?" Cora asked, as her energy level and interest were dramatically raised.

"I'm afraid not. What's it like?"

Cora was excited to share with Josh's mom the history of The Del. She described the architecture and even mentioned the haunted stories of Kate Morgan. His mom was fascinated and hung on Cora's every word. Josh was interested until his dad came down for breakfast. They started in on the business while Cora enchanted his mom with countless stories. It felt good for Cora to talk about The Del. She decided against sharing her experience with Kate, thinking she might get judged as being crazy. Plus, it was too personal and special to Cora. It was better to keep it all safely locked away.

After breakfast, Josh and Cora headed to the barn. Josh saddled up a brown mare for Cora. He kept throwing around words like 'side saddle', 'English' and 'western'. She had no idea what he was talking about. Her horse looked about as disinterested in the whole process as Cora felt. At least it didn't appear wild or unruly. Cora was starting to wonder why she agreed to going riding in the first place. In contrast, Josh looked fairly content with the unfolding events. His horse was ready in no time. He helped Cora mount her beast and then jumped on his. Cora took the reins in her hands, completely unsure what to do with them. Josh's mom gave her a few tips, like pretending to be confident to fool the horse, leaning back in the saddle and that it was all about being relaxed. Cora was wobbly at first, but caught on fairly quick. Her horse got in line behind Josh's and ignored Cora.

"You alright back there?" Josh called out to Cora.

"Couldn't be better," Cora said as she rolled her eyes.

After Cora became adjusted to the horse ride, she turned her focus to her surroundings. They were traveling along a dirt trail south of the house. It was fairly flat before it ascended into the foothills. There was a light frost on the ground, as the sun hadn't come up yet to melt it away. Cora was glad she borrowed the thick winter jacket Josh's mom offered her earlier in the morning. Cora's nose was already frozen and even her fingers were still cold in her leather gloves. Josh was oblivious to it all. In fact, it all seemed to excite him. Perhaps Cora should have had a second cup of coffee; maybe it would have improved her sour mood.

As the sun came closer to making its daily appearance, the sky started to slowly lighten. It was so gradual that Cora barely noticed the change until the hue of blackish gray turned to a deep blue, then a lighter blue into an orangish red. Seemingly out of nowhere, the edge of the sun was visible. The few clouds in the sky lit up like huge red cotton balls. Cora welcomed the warmth on her face. With the arrival of the sun, everything started to come alive. Birds began socializing with each other through song. The grasses swayed when little bunnies and rodents ran by. Even the horses were perkier. Cora was almost beginning to enjoy the ride.

The day before, Josh mentioned riding to the back 40, but Cora didn't know what that meant.

"How far are we going?" Cora asked Josh.

"Once we reach the trees, it's about 10 miles up over the ridge."

This piece of information wasn't very helpful. Since Cora had never ridden a horse, she wasn't sure how long ten miles would take. She was already tired of looking stupid so she remained quiet.

Cora lost track of time as they journeyed on. She forgot to wear her watch since she was only half awake when Josh got her out of bed. She was beginning to track the journey through her sore muscles. Her rear was the first to feel the effects of the ride. The up and down movements were taking their toll. The next muscles to scream out were her thighs and then the rest of her leg muscles joined in the protest. Cora wasn't sure how much longer her body would last before it gave out. She was relieved when she spotted a small log cabin. It had to be where they were headed. Josh dismounted and then assisted Cora.

"This cabin was built by my great-grandfather back in 1874," Josh said proudly.

"The logs must have been cut by hand. I can't imagine how long it took."

"When he bought this land, he lived right here with my great-grandmother. They put the house close to the river. Back in the day, you needed to be close to a water source. We forget about that with wells and piping available to us now," Josh prattled on.

"There is so much history here." Cora said, looking

around.

"It is where I come from, Cora. My roots. It means a lot to me," Josh replied.

"I can see that," Cora said as she stretched her muscles.

"You ready for some cowboy grub?"

"I sure am. I am famished."

"Let's go see what's cooking," Josh said as they headed toward the cabin.

The inside of the log cabin was dark. Although there were windows, there were just a few of them and they were fairly small. The stove had a large pot cooking on it and something smelled delicious.

"It looks like beef stew. Grab a bowl and dish yourself some up," Josh said as he stirred the stew.

Cora filled a bowl brimming with the beef, potatoes, carrots and gravy. It actually tasted even better than it smelled. Soon after she began eating, Josh left to go speak with his dad. He didn't come back, so Cora kept herself busy by snooping around the cabin. She was intrigued by the old books and spent a fair amount of time perusing them. She sat on the couch, closed her eyes and instantly fell asleep. She awoke to Josh's kiss and his face upon hers.

"You look so peaceful when you sleep. I hated to wake you, but we need to get going in order to make it back before dark. Plus, I have a stop I want to make."

Cora was not thrilled about getting back on the horse, but she was looking forward to a long soak in a very hot bath. They rode for over an hour until Josh dismounted near a slow moving stream. He assisted Cora off the horse and then pulled a blanket out of his satchel. He laid it in a grassy area under a patch of almost naked birch trees. The yellow leaves already on the ground provided an extra soft layer of comfort. Cora was quick to lie down and stretch her muscles. Josh brought out a flask from his other satchel. It was filled with nice cool water.

"Would you like some water?"

"I am ready for my kiss," Josh said as he pulled Cora in for a kiss. Cora wasn't in the mood; however, Josh was definitely in the mood. He slipped his hand up Cora's shirt and unhooked her bra. His hand swept across her nipples. He pulled her shirt up to expose her breasts to the sun. He licked the area around her nipple and then kissed the cleavage to make sure it didn't feel left out. Cora tried to get in the mood. It had been a few weeks since she was intimate with Josh, but her body was not cooperating. She was sore from head to toe and the last thing she felt like doing was having sex. Josh obviously felt differently. He wanted some and he wanted it now. Great! Just what Cora needed in this moment was another unfulfilling sexual experience.

She knew how it worked with most men. Their number one goal was to please themselves. If they pleased the woman, then it was an added bonus. But if they didn't, quite honestly, she wasn't sure what they thought. She had been with so many boys that thought they were men; as long as they had their ejaculation, it was considered good sex and time to roll over. They would grab the woman by the butt and assume this turned her on. Then they would skip right to intercourse, drill it in, and then release. After the ten minutes, they would give the girl a kiss and say, "Was that good for you baby?" The only kind response was, "Yes." However, if the guy had an ounce of a brain, he would realize that the woman was completely not into it. Cora was beginning to wonder if that was the extent of sex. Perhaps that is why toys were really invented; to finish off where the guy couldn't.

While Josh had his way with her, Cora looked up at the clouds. It was quite beautiful lying on a blanket out in the open. The soft breeze blowing across her nipples felt like the wind was licking her to arousal. Cora closed her eyes and enjoyed the sensation of being partially naked under the sun. A smile crossed her face as she remembered Brent's thigh touching hers in the spa. She wondered if Brent found her touch exciting. Passion soared through her when she imagined Brent's hand reaching down her thigh and touching her soft, warm spot. It thrilled her to imagine Brent grabbing her hair and pulling her in for a kiss. She could almost feel his tongue teasing her, giving her just enough to want more, much more. Her body groaned and yearned for Brent's. It reacted to his imaginary touch.

"Honey, you are so hot right now. You must really want some," Josh said, filled with excitement.

Josh's voice jolted Cora out of her fantasy with Brent. What was she doing thinking about Brent as Josh was being passionate with her? Cora wondered if it was common for a woman to think about another man when they were having sex with their boyfriend. Was thinking about it just as bad as doing it? Cora was so turned on thinking about Brent that she rationalized that other unsatisfied women had to be doing this as well. Cora got so wet thinking about Brent, yet with Josh, the excitement level was not quite the same. What did it all mean?

Before Cora could think that much about it all, Josh was groaning and shouting out Cora's name. His release came fast and hard. His hot sweaty body fell limp on top of Cora. She played with his hair as he lay still across her. She felt a sweetness that caused her to smile. Josh was a really good guy. She was lucky to be with someone so kind and considerate. Their love life didn't have to be passionate. It was comforting to be with someone so consistent. She knew what to expect from Josh. It was enough for Cora. It had to be.

When they arrived back at the barn, Cora could barely walk. She hobbled into the house and went straight to the bathroom. Josh went with her, helped get her set up for her soak and left her alone to enjoy her bath. She put in extra bubbles, wishing away the sore muscles. She lay in the tub for over an hour. When the water became the slightest bit cool, she emptied out some and added piping hot water. She deserved it and wasn't going to move until she had enough. She closed her eyes and let all of her worries just fall off of her. She took life a little too seriously at times. She needed to learn how to relax and just go with the flow. Cora closed her eyes and finished her earlier sexual thoughts about Brent.

After her pleasureful bath, Cora checked her emails. She told herself it was to see if her roommate or her mother wrote, but she knew deep down that she was checking to see if Brent responded to her email. She was disappointed when there was no message from Brent. She wasn't sure what she was expecting, but hearing from him felt good, probably too good.

Cora could barely keep her eyes open the rest of the evening. She went to bed fairly early. She knew if she was sore from her horse ride in the evening, the morning would only be worse. She was hoping that a few extra hours of sleep might help. She wasn't 100% sure what it would help, but she was willing to try anything.

Chapter 8

The sun was up when Cora woke up the next day. It was the day before Thanksgiving. She felt terrible. She could barely walk over to the bathroom. She couldn't remember ever being so sore and had no interest in sitting in any chair at this point. She wasn't sure if she should climb back into bed or try walking around. Josh's mom made the decision for her.

"Hi, dear. How are you feeling? Josh thought you might be a little sore today. Here is some ointment you can rub on your muscles. Once you feel like it, just come on downstairs and we can begin the meal preparations for our Thanksgiving dinner tomorrow," Josh's mom said, handing Cora the ointment.

"Thank you," were the only words Cora could muster up. She totally forgot that Josh had volunteered her to help with the Thanksgiving meal. Cora rubbed the ointment over most of her body. It helped some, but her muscles were still terribly achy. Cora got dressed and went downstairs to help with the meal preparations.

The day went faster than Cora imagined. Josh's mom was fun to be around. She gave Cora all of the easy jobs once she realized that Cora wouldn't be that great of a helper. Cora became her prep cook that cut, chopped and then washed dishes. In actuality, it was a lot of help for Josh's mom. Plus, she enjoyed the company. With both of her kids grown and out of the house, Cora could tell that she was lonely. She felt a little sorry for her. She definitely needed someone to interact with and Josh's dad did not appear to be into interacting with anyone unless it was about the business.

Thanksgiving came and brought with it more people that Cora didn't know. Josh was the proper boyfriend and stayed by her side throughout the day. He introduced her to everyone and spoke very highly of her work and future plans. It was sweet to see Josh dote on her. She enjoyed the attention. There was little talk of the business. It was a day meant for family and Cora felt a part of it all. She barely thought of Brent, until she checked her email after dinner and read his latest message that he sent earlier in the day:

Corina,

Are you leaving the company? Your email was so formal and sounded like a letter of resignation. My mother mentioned that you might be moving to another company. Please come see me before you make any decisions.

Happy Thanksgiving, Corina! May you be surrounded by love on this special holiday.

Brent

P.S. It is the anniversary of Kate's passing. I wonder if she is roaming the halls of The Del tonight.

Brent's mother was a liar and relentless. She seemed determined to move Cora out of the company as quickly as possible. Or was it something else? Did she want to distance Cora away from Brent? But why? Cora couldn't compare to Grace. She didn't even come close. What was his mother's problem? Cora was irritated. Nobody was going to run her out of any job. She had a tremendous opportunity at Locke Incorporated and she wasn't about to leave it until she was ready. Cora quickly composed herself so she could respond to Brent's email and return to the Thanksgiving gathering:

Brent,

I have no intentions of leaving your company. I am sorry if I left your mother with that impression. Quite the contrary, I am thankful for the trust you put in me when Julie could not oversee the conference. I enjoyed the experience and know it will serve me well in my career. I want to learn as much as I can at Locke Incorporated. I would like to stay as long as you feel I can serve the needs of the company.

I hope you enjoy your Thanksgiving. I am not with my family, but am surrounded by a wonderful family that cares a lot for one another. I miss my grandmother and hope to be able to see her within the coming year. We spoke today and she is doing well.

I don't know how to put this into words, but Kate was in my room the night of the luau. I realize that this is hard to believe, but it is true. She never spoke a word; however, she led me to the place where she died. Remember when you showed me the location? I am unsure what she wanted me to understand, but it was one of the most intriguing experiences in my life. I wasn't going to tell anyone about it, but I felt you might understand.

Sincerely,

Cora

Cora sent the message before she thought too much about it and chickened out. She wasn't sure why she told Brent about Kate. He probably would just brush it off as nonsense. He had spent enough time around Cora to know that she was a little silly at times.
Cora did miss her grandmother. She was hoping to be able to save enough money to go see her in the summer. It felt so long from then, but it was the only option at the moment. The only reason she was able to fly to Montana was because Josh had some frequent flyer miles for her to use. It was painful not having any money. Perhaps that would change over time; being broke was not fun.

After finishing her email to Brent, Cora went downstairs for dessert. She was ready for a huge helping of pumpkin pie. She wanted to get to bed early. Cora was still not able to convince Josh to spend the day in Glacier National Park, but it didn't deter Cora. Josh's mom was willing to lend her the car to make the journey. Cora didn't think she would be back in Montana anytime soon, so she decided to take advantage of the opportunity. Josh was riding out to the back 40 again and there was no way Cora was going to accompany him.

Cora got an early start on Friday. After receiving countless recommendations from Josh's mom, Cora headed out. Even though it was the end of November, all of the roads in Glacier National Park were passable. The area had some snow earlier in the month, but due to the unseasonably warm weather, most of it had already melted. The car had 4-wheel drive so she was set.

The entrance to the park was fairly close to Columbia Falls. Cora took the Going-to-the-Sun road. She thought that was a pretty awesome name for a road. Cora's first stop was the Lake McDonald Valley. The valley contained a glassy lake enclosed by snow-kissed mountains. The park brochure stated that the lake was ten miles long and 500 feet deep. It was the largest lake in the park. Cora stayed at the overlook for a few minutes to embed the scene in her memory. She often took mental pictures that she could call on when she needed something good in her life. Once she had it all captured, she jumped back in the car. She wanted to spend as much time as possible in Waterton, Canada. Josh's mom said that Waterton contained the gem of the park. She wouldn't tell Cora exactly what it was, but said that when Cora saw it, she would know. Cora moved on in the park and drove through Logan Pass, but did not stop. When she reached the St. Mary Valley, she had to take a closer look. In the valley, the open meadows converged with the dense forest. The lake sat right in the middle of it all. Cora pondered how the whole valley was formed so long ago.

Cora turned on Chief Mountain International Highway and headed toward Canada. Everywhere she gazed, she found nothing but natural untouched beauty. The solitude of this trip gave Cora plenty of time to mull things over. She needed to face the doubts she was having about her relationship with Josh. There was no question that they were really good friends. She thought they knew a lot about each other, but Cora was seeing another and very different side to Josh: his country side. Unfortunately, it wasn't anything that Cora could relate to, and she wasn't very interested in becoming a part of it. He was passionate about land, animals and country life, while Cora gained her strength from the hustle and bustle of the city. There were also some other concerns.

After spending time with Brent, Cora realized she wanted the man to be the leader in the relationship. While she was a capable decision maker, she didn't want to do it all the time. It felt good when someone else stood up and took charge of a situation. It enabled her to sit back and relax. What a concept! Josh was very laid back and went with the flow. Occasionally, he would get an idea and make something happen, like their tourist date in San Francisco, but those occurrences were rare. If Cora wanted something to happen, she usually had to do it herself.

After a beautiful drive, Cora arrived at her destination - the town of Waterton. She immediately fell in love with the charm of the place. She decided to walk though the downtown area and find a coffee shop. She wondered if the gem of the park that Josh's mom referred to was simply the overall vibe of the quaint town. Yet his mom said she would just know, and so far that wasn't happening. Cora found a sweet little coffee shop and entered. The cashier was very friendly.

"Is this your first time in Waterton?" The cashier asked cheerfully.

"Is it that obvious?" Cora laughed.

"The park map in your hand is a dead giveaway."

"I heard that Waterton contains the gem of Glacier National Park, but I can't figure out what that means."

"Would you like a little help?"

"Please. I only have a limited amount of time to see it all," Cora said, happy to have a little help.

The cashier gave Cora detailed directions and set her on her way. Cora was enjoying her day's adventure. It didn't take long for Cora to find the mystery she was seeking. Right before her eyes was the most enchanting scene. A picturesque European style hotel sat on top of a hill overlooking a pristine crystal blue lake. Cora pulled over to the side of the road to take a few pictures with her cell phone camera. She had never seen anything quite like it. She wondered if Brent had been there. It seemed like a place he would visit. On a whim, she sent a picture message with no text of the hotel to Brent. After she sent it, she felt a little foolish. There was something about the man that caused her to do crazy things and then instantly regret them. Moments later, her phone vibrated.

It was a text from Brent, 'The Prince of Wales Hotel. Bruce has more class than I gave him credit.'

Cora laughed. How many times did she have to correct him?

She texted back, 'Josh (not Bruce) is back at the ranch. I am out exploring by myself.'

Brent replied, 'Cora the explorer. Are you staying the night at the Prince of Wales? It is a must.'

Cora laughed again. 'Lol. My boss doesn't pay me enough to afford such luxury.'

Brent replied, 'Maybe if you worked harder, you'd get paid more. Instead of ditching work, you are out gallivanting in the mountains.'

Cora was braver with Brent when he wasn't standing in front of her. She wrote, 'It sounds like you miss me. Who else do you have to pick on?'

'I am saving all my nastiness for your return on Monday.' Cora was surprised that he knew she was returning on Monday. He must need something, she rationalized.

Before Cora could reply, Brent wrote again, 'If you keep being bad, I'm going to take back the thank you gift I placed on your desk.'

'I'll be good, I promise.' Cora quickly texted back.

'What is your definition of good, Corina?' Brent responded.

'First tell me what the gift is so I can determine if it is worth being good.'

'Nice try, but I don't want to spoil the opening of your gift. You should probably go on and finish enjoying your ditch day expedition. Somebody needs to work and since you're not here, I have to be sure everyone here picks up your slack.'

'Yes, Sir. I will be sure to have fun for the both of us.' Cora replied.

'Don't have too much fun, Corina.'

Too much fun? Cora wasn't sure what he meant by that comment but she was smiling and thoroughly enjoyed her bantering and flirtatious communication with this challenging man.

Cora put her phone away and got back into the car. She drove to the hotel to take a closer look at the "gem". She went inside and read a little history about the place. It was built in 1926. The construction was difficult due to the location and inclement weather. The project was almost abandoned due to extremely high winds. However, the owner persevered and the 86 room hotel was completed. It stood seven stories high and boasted a 30 foot bell tower. The architecture was modeled after French and Swiss chalets. It was named after Prince Edward, who was adored by the people at that time. He was highly respected even though he married an American commoner.

Cora loved the description of Prince Edward's private life; nothing like still being respected even though you stooped so low as to marry below your class grade. Cora doubted that Brent's mother would have approved if Brent married a girl below his level in society. Most likely, Grace had all the correct aristocratic societal papers to meet Brent's mother's approval. Cora just couldn't stop the green monster of jealousy from rearing its ugly head when it came to Grace.

In an attempt to redirect the jealous thoughts from her mind, she went up to the hotel restaurant and ordered some lunch. Cora took a seat by the window, stared out at the lake and wondered how on such a gorgeous day in a beautiful environment, she decided to reach out to Brent to share her adventure with a text photo instead of Josh. The signs that she and Josh were not a good match were everywhere. It was unsettling. Just last week, she gave her heart to a man who was unavailable and now she was contemplating breaking up with a man who would keep her heart safe yet unfulfilled. It looked like Cora was going to be alone; however, she would rather be alone than with the wrong person. It wasn't fair to her and it surely wasn't fair to Josh.

Cora's fun day of solitude was now turning serious. Before making the return trip to the ranch, Cora took a walk outside of the hotel after her lunch to stretch her legs. The air was colder than when she first arrived in Waterton. Clouds were moving in quickly, blocking the warmth of the sun. Cora could tell that it was about to snow.

Growing up, Cora learned that snow provides many small cues that it is on the way. As clouds gather, they carry a distinct whiteness to them. It is like the snow making machines are in full speed, churning up the clouds to remove the impurities. It is a cleansing of the sky. Another clue is a distinct smell in the air. It is a "crisp innocent clarity" that permeates everything. You can practically cut the air with scissors; it is so crisp. Cora's intuition was validated when she saw the first snowflake. It dropped down in front of her and melted in her hand. Before she knew it, the snowflake had many friends falling from the sky. The snow began to softly sit upon all it touched as if to say, "Rest now. I am here."

Just then Cora became a bit anxious with thoughts of being able to drive to the ranch safely. She quickly decided that it would be best to get going. Cora started her walk back to the car, telling herself she would make it back to the ranch without any problems. As she walked, she stopped and took a quick picture of the hotel with the newly formed thin layer of snow all around it. The large expansive branches of the trees once dark green were now sprinkled with powdery snow sugar. They looked like gigantic sugar cookies all lined up in a winter wonderland. She thought maybe she would send the picture to Brent later.

Before starting the car, Cora took a moment to look

out the car windows and take in the beauty of the snowfall. The snow looked much less threatening from the inside of the car as it brought a peaceful serenity everywhere it landed. The snow rested easily upon a telephone wire and placed itself delicately on the needles of the pine trees. Cora wondered with so many various snowflakes swirling in the air, how did they all find just the perfect spot? When they come from the sky, are they dancing around in joy or do they fall with fear to the ground? There are so many mysteries in nature with so few answers, thought Cora.

The drive back to the ranch took longer than expected. The snow caused everyone to be more cautious. Cora texted Josh to let him know that she was safe and would be back in the evening. It seemed fitting to listen to Enya's music, "The Memory of Trees", on the car's CD player as she carefully drove through the raw natural park surrounding the road. A winter wonderland was unfolding right in front her as she drove. The beauty of the music and beauty of her surroundings reached far into Cora's heart. She felt profoundly touched, and in this moment, all was right in her world. Her concerns about her relationship with Josh, inappropriate attraction for Brent, and flailing career path simply slipped away.

The suddenness of the snowfall was a reminder that although things can appear one way, in an instant, they can change and be completely different. Cora had a strength within herself that was not dependent on circumstances. She was a competent woman, able to stand alone, if that was her destiny. She had a purpose in life and she was determined to discover and fulfill it.

She wouldn't change herself to mold into someone else's vision for her life. If she did, she would be living their life and not her own. She was not a country girl and she didn't want to become one, now or ever. She had nothing against those that did, but she was wired differently. Josh was born and raised on the family ranch and would most likely want to return to it someday. Cora had no intention of living her life on an isolated piece of land far from the energy of a city. She really cared for Josh, but she could not sacrifice her dreams for his. Perhaps this is what people did when they were in love, but Cora did not have feelings strong enough for Josh to take that step. Tears streamed down her face as she realized what it all meant: she was going to break up with Josh. He was an incredible guy, however, it was not going to work out.

Cora was revitalized and resolved to take action as she arrived back at the ranch. Josh's mom had a plate of dinner ready for her when she walked in to the kitchen. Cora thanked her profusely for the meal and lending her the car.

"I had so much fun today. Thank you for making it special," Cora said as she hugged Josh's mom.

"You're welcome. Did you find the gem?"

"Did I ever! The Prince of Wales hotel is simply remarkable. It reminded me a little of the Hotel del Coronado. The history is so rich and the beauty unmatched. I find it difficult to put in words."

"I knew you'd enjoy it. We love the beauty of Montana,

and we have some exceptional tourist spots here as well."

"You sure do. When it started to snow, I was a little concerned at first, but once I knew I was safe, I thoroughly enjoyed the magic of the snow," Cora said as her eyes grew bright with excitement.

Josh meandered into the kitchen and joined the conversation, "Mom is right. There is no other place in the world like Columbia Falls, Montana. It means so much to me that you recognize its uniqueness." Josh bent down and kissed her.

Cora sensed where the conversation was going, but did not want to have it in front of his mom.

Josh then added, "I can't believe we fly back tomorrow. I didn't know how much I missed it until I was here again. I'm not ready to face all the traffic and people in San Francisco. Isn't it great to escape all of that, Cora?"

"Yes, it is nice here," Cora said quietly. "But I love the energy in the Bay Area. It's fun to explore new places, but Berkeley is my home. It makes me who I am."

Josh was silent. Cora knew that they would eventually have the discussion, but Josh was obviously not ready. She didn't want to rush him. She had already made her decision and nothing was going to change her mind.

The next day, Josh was fairly quiet. His parents were also somber. Many hugs and kisses were exchanged at the airport. Cora hid her growing excitement to return home. She wanted to respect Josh's feelings. It was difficult to leave home. Cora now understood that Josh's home was in Montana and hers was in the Bay Area.

When they were on the plane, Josh spent the majority of his time staring out the window. Cora reached over and placed her hand in his.

"How are you doing?" Cora asked gently.

It took awhile for Josh to respond. "I'm okay."

"It's hard for you to leave it all behind, isn't it? Is that why you don't visit more often?"

Josh's voice shook when he responded, "Yes."

"Why don't you move back home? I've never seen you so alive and engaged as you have been this past week," Cora asked as she brushed his cheek with her hand.

"I want to. There is just one thing standing in my way," Josh said staring intently at Cora.

"Is it your job? I'm sure your dad could use some extra help on the ranch or maybe another ranch nearby."

Josh grabbed both of Cora's hands in his, "You don't get it do you?"

Cora was perplexed, "No, I don't."

"It's you, Cora. Why do you think I wanted you to

come to the ranch? I wanted you to fall in love with it the way I do, but it didn't happen."

"Oh Josh. It was wonderful. I can see why you are so drawn to it," Cora said feeling bad that she didn't have any reassurance to offer him.

"But?" Josh asked.

"But it isn't somewhere I want to live," Cora responded softly.

"Even for me?" Josh asked.

"I thought a lot about it yesterday and as much as I care for you, I cannot give up my dreams for yours."

"Then I will give up mine to be with you. Cora, I love you," Josh said.

"Josh, I can't let you do that for me. It wouldn't be right. Over time you would grow to resent me and I don't want that for either of us. It is hard to let you go, but there is no way I can allow you to stay in California for me," Cora said as she started to cry. There was no way she was going to move to Montana, but she was really close to Josh and he provided stability in her life.

"See, this is why my mom likes you so much. You're so thoughtful," Josh said.

"I like her a lot to. She is an incredible woman."

"So what does this mean for us? Don't you love me?"

"Honestly, I don't know how I feel. I do know that my home is in the Bay Area. My future and career are there. Does this make me a bad person?" Cora asked.

"This is not how I expected this week to turn out. I should have never cornered you into going in the first place. If I had left it alone, we would be fine right now," Josh said as he pulled away from Cora. He was hurt and Cora didn't know how to reach him.
She was a little surprised how strongly she felt about the whole situation. It started for her before the trip to Montana. In fact, it started when she first got to know Brent. When she was with Brent, she felt like she could just be herself. It felt good to just be instead of pretending to be what someone else wanted. Even though she couldn't have Brent, he showed her there was someone out there that fit her needs. He gave her hope.

"Josh, we wouldn't have been fine. Life is too short to ignore our hearts' desires. We each have a destiny that we are born with. So many people ignore their purpose in life and just settle on how things are. I saw how much you love the family ranching business. You can't get enough of it. You were born into it. Stop fighting it. If our paths are meant to cross again, they will," Cora said as she hugged Josh.

"Did we just break up?" Josh asked.

"Yes, I think we did."

"Cora, this isn't over. I love you. In time, you will

realize that you love me too. I am not letting you go just like that. I am going to fight for us," Josh said as he put her hand to his heart.

"I can't let you do that. In time, you will see that this is for the best," Cora said tenderly.

Josh did not reply.

The ride back to Cora's apartment was tense. She was grateful when Josh didn't ask to come in and talk. She had enough talking for one day. Her roommate, Lynn, was out so Cora had the place to herself. Cora put her suitcase next to her luggage from The Del. The last two weeks had been a whirlwind. She was ready for some familiar routine.

Later in the evening, Cora's phone beeped. She did not want to talk to anyone. She smiled slightly when she saw it was a text from Brent.

'I have a lot of work for you on Monday; you better rest up.'

Cora couldn't help but laugh. Although the man was a tyrant, she was glad to have his friendship.

Cora replied, 'Yes, Boss. I will be sure to be in bed at 8pm tomorrow night. Is this acceptable?'

Brent wrote back, 'Submission will get you everywhere, Corina.'

Cora wrote, 'I will be sure to remember that advice, Mr. Locke.'

'Sarcasm will get you nowhere," Brent retorted.

Just when she thought she was winning, he one upped her. During her textual banter with Brent, she received a text from Josh.

'Have you gone to bed? If not, I would like to talk some more,' wrote Josh. Cora rolled her eyes. The last thing she felt like doing was rehashing the draining conversation from the plane ride home.

Cora wrote back to Josh, 'I think we need to let some time pass before we talk again.'

Cora received another text from Brent, 'Was it something I said?'

What was Brent talking about, Cora wondered? She looked at her text history and realized she sent the text for Josh to Brent. Why was she so apt to screw things up around Brent? She quickly shot another text to Brent.

'Oops, I meant to send the last text to my boyfriend. Sorry for the confusion.'

Brent replied, 'Trouble in paradise?'

Cora giggled. Brent was pretty witty. She responded, 'You could say that.'

Brent responded, 'Bruce in the doghouse?'

Cora wrote back, 'More like on the ranch. Long story.'
Brent replied, 'I have time.'

Cora wondered what Grace and his children were
doing. He seemed sincere about listening to her story,
but it wasn't appropriate. She was supposed to be
putting a professional distance between them before
she acted on her feelings for him.

She texted back, 'Thanks. Maybe another time.'

Brent wrote, 'Okay. See you on Monday.'

Chapter 9

Sunday was a blur. Cora talked to Josh a few times, but nothing changed. Her roommate, Lynn listened to Cora's catch-up story on work, Montana and the latest with Josh and then gave her own take on the situation. None of the conversational observations that Lynn provided made Cora feel any better. By the time Sunday evening rolled around, Cora was actually looking forward to going to work. She wanted to get past all the sadness as quick as possible. Plus, she was curious about the surprise thank you gift sitting on her desk and wanted to share Waterton stories with Brent. When Cora walked into the office on Monday morning, Brent came out to meet her.

"Back to the salt mines, Cora. I have a lot I need you to do for me today."

"Okay. Let me put down my purse and I will meet you in your office," Cora said.

"I can provide you with a list of the projects," Brent said, as he followed Cora to her desk.

In the middle of Cora's desk was an envelope with 'CORINA' written on the front in bold letters.

"Is it my pink slip?" Cora nervously asked.

"Why the doubt and fear, Cora? Open it," Brent directed.

Cora slowly opened the envelope. It held a few pieces of paper. Cora was shocked when she realized it was a round trip ticket to fly to New York at Christmas. Tears welled up in her eyes. Cora looked up at Brent.

"This is the nicest thing anyone has ever done for me."

"Cora, you deserve it. It was my first international conference as CEO of Locke, Incorporated. When Julie told me she couldn't attend, my heart sank. I didn't take any part in the planning, which was a huge mistake on my part. You were my only hope. Julie was confident that you could do it. You saved me at the last minute. You surprised me that you stepped up and made it happen. I felt bad that I laid all the pressure of such an important event on an intern, my favorite intern. But Julie and I really believed you could step in and deliver. Thank you, Corina."

Brent moved in close, put his arms around Cora and pulled her into an embrace. Cora's knees went weak when her face brushed against his. She could smell his masculine scent and it drove her wild. A man's smell was critical for Cora and his was just right! His arms were strong around her small frame. She wanted to stay in the embrace forever. She felt invincible.

Brent slowly pulled back and said, "Now go call your

grandmother and tell her the good news."

"Oh, yes," Cora stammered. "Thank you, Brent."

"You're welcome, Corina," Brent said as he walked away.

Cora immediately called her grandmother to let her know that she would be visiting in just a few weeks. She kept the call short because she didn't want to press her luck.

Throughout the day, the office staff came to congratulate Cora on the success of the conference. Julie was by far the proudest.

"Cora, you are amazing! I knew you could do it. Brent has been talking non-stop about how productive the conference was for the business and the environmental industry as a whole. He mentioned something about you turning water into wine at the luau," Julie laughed as she hugged Cora.

Cora was confused. "I don't know what he is referring to with the wine."

"Sweetie, I am just messing with you. I have never seen Brent so complimentary of one of his employees. You better watch out, some of the other ladies are going to become jealous of all the attention you are receiving from the boss," Julie cautioned her with a straight face.

"Should I be concerned?" Cora said, instantly worried.

"Girl, take it down a notch. I am just messing with you. Don't get all serious on me. Hey, I forgot to ask, how was Montana? Did you have any good ranch romping or barn haystack details that you need to tell me about?" Julie asked as she made herself comfortable on Cora's desk.

"Seriously?" Cora sometimes wondered who the supervisor was in their relationship.

"If I didn't want to know, I wouldn't have asked. Details. Now."

Cora told Julie the short version of her trip to Montana, some of the revelations she came to at Glacier National Park, and the break-up with Josh. Cora asked Julie not to tell anyone. She wasn't ready for the sympathy or the fix-ups. Julie processed it all and gave Cora a supportive hug. It was harder than she realized to talk about it. Cora felt bad about hurting Josh and hearing the story out loud made her feel even worse.

Later in the day, Cora asked Julie a little about Grace. "What can you tell me about Grace Locke?"

Julie's face brightened. "Did you meet her? Isn't she incredible? Her name is so fitting to her personality."

"No, but Brent's mother, Leslie, couldn't stop talking about her. She must be an interesting mother-in-law for Grace. I got the distinct feeling that Brent's mother did not like me one bit."

"Really? She can be direct, but she's been really kind to

me," Julie said, a little surprised. Direct? More like harshly direct truth bender, thought Cora.

"Maybe she just doesn't like interns," Cora laughed.

"She does tend to lean more towards the blue blood girls of high society," Julie said.

"Like Grace?" Cora asked.

"Do I sense a little resentment toward Grace?" Julie inquired.

"No. Well, maybe a little. She is drop-dead gorgeous, connected, confident, self-assured…." Cora went on and on.

"Really? How do you know all of this if you haven't even spoken to her?" Julie asked.

"Fine. I may be projecting a little."

"A little?" Julie scolded Cora.

"Well, you can't deny that she is a sexy woman that oozes class out of every pearl around her dainty neck," Cora said, with bit of jealousy in her voice.

"Okay, let's say I agree with your description. How would you describe yourself?"

"Myself? You mean me," Cora asked, as she brought up her shoulders, raised her nose and squinted her eyes to better understand Julie's question.

"Yes. How do you describe yourself?" Julie said, with her arms folded.

"Fine. I am a nice person. I have pretty eyes. My legs are alright. How's that Julie?"

"Cora, you've got to be kidding. That's it? That's how you see yourself?"

"I'm getting better at dressing, thanks to the clothes you lent me for the conference," responded Cora.

"I give up," Julie said, as she threw her hands up in the air.

"Is she being difficult again, Julie?" Brent asked, as he popped out of his office to join in on the conversation.

"Yes. I am glad you are here, Brent. I need a man's perspective. Could you provide me with one sentence that accurately describes Cora?" Julie said smirking. Cora was mortified.

"She's just joking, Brent. Please don't answer her," Cora pleaded.

"Cora, I am sorry, but I wouldn't dream of passing up an opportunity to weigh-in on this! Let's see, one sentence. Cora is a passionate competent woman who brings joy to those around her. She minimizes her own talents and unique beauty, which makes her even more alluring," Brent said as he stared directly into Cora's eyes. Julie, Brent and Cora were quiet for what felt like an eternity to Cora. The sexual tension was palpable.

Cora, with her heart pounding, finally whispered, "That's two sentences."

Julie quickly added, "Thanks Brent. I knew you could help". Julie, now satisfied, looked at her watch and realized she had to leave for a meeting. "I'm going to see if the final figures from the hotel expenses are in from the conference."

Brent remained and had yet to drop his gaze from Cora's. His arms were folded across his chest. "Is the truth difficult for you to hear, Cora?"

"No. Yes. I don't know," Cora stammered.

Brent tossed his head back and smiled from ear to ear. "You are too much fun. Your honesty is so refreshing. Next Friday, I am headed out to Napa for a quick business meeting. After the meeting, I am going to select the company's annual wines as a part of the employee Christmas bonus. I want you to join me at 10:00am at the Mondavi Vineyards. You can help me make the wine selections. Just drive directly there on next Friday; you don't need to come to the office first. I already notified Julie. Now, back to work, Corina," Brent said as he disappeared again.

The man was skilled at quickly weaving in and out of conversations. He didn't sit still for long. Spending the day in Napa with Brent sounded fun, yet dangerous. Cora's feelings for the man were not diminishing; they were only growing stronger. She was still in shock from the generous thank you gift. He remembered their conversation about how much it meant for Cora to spend time with her grandma. There weren't many men that would be so thoughtful. It wasn't the amount of money that it cost for the ticket; it was the sentimental thought behind it which meant so much to her. Cora had it bad for the man. She was going to need to do something to squelch the feelings rapidly expanding in her heart. They were growing deeper by the day.

Cora was still walking on clouds by the time she made it home to her apartment. She was looking forward to a relaxing soak in the tub. At precisely 7:00pm, her phone rang. She knew it was Josh. It was their nightly ritual, one she was already beginning to slightly miss. Cora stuck to her guns and did not answer the phone. It was for the best. She felt lousy for ignoring the call, but she needed to be firm.

Throughout the course of the rest of the week, Josh continued to call and Cora continued to not answer. The messages Josh left were sweet and tugged at Cora's heart. By the end of the week, she was questioning if she was doing the right thing. Her reasons for letting Josh go were beginning to get a little blurry in her mind. They had shared some fun times together. Cora was not sure what to do so she stuck to her original plan and kept her distance.

Friday finally arrived. It was a normal work day filled with routine issues, dilemmas, and plenty of monotony. As she puttered through her day, her blue eyes constantly moved toward the window. While her body went through the motions of working, her spirit was already joyfully frolicking outside, soaking in the sunlight. It was lunch time when she finally cut the restrictive strings of responsibility and escaped out of the building. She slowly wandered down the street in search of a place to break away and feel life.

The sun was just as warm and inviting as it had appeared from her office window. She found a nice table outside of a sandwich shop to sit alone with her thoughts. People were busy socializing, laughing and participating in their own little worlds. She was content to sit and watch them; the observer is always treated to a show if they can patiently sit and follow where their attention goes, she reminded herself.

After awhile, the conversations began to blend and swirl into the soothing background. The instrumental music from some outdoor speakers took center stage and infiltrated her thoughts. She was drawn back to Brent. Lately, it seemed to all trail back to him. Each note of the song was a step back to a memory they shared. The power of the memory enticed her to savor it again and again and again. This time, her memory brought her to the time they spent together at the Hotel del Coronado. She was swept away by the memory of the ocean, the breeze running through his hair, his smile, the shape of his lips. She imagined him pulling her in close for a tender kiss.

Cora shook her head as she chastised herself. She had to stop fantasizing about her boss, her married boss. What happened to her morals?

When she arrived back at the office, she heard a familiar voice greet her.

"Cora, it is so nice to see you. How are you?" Brent's dad, Robert Locke, said as he hugged her tightly. Cora's face lit up. It felt wonderful to see such a friendly face. She did feel a little guilty that she was just fantasizing about his son.

"Mr. Locke, what a nice surprise! Are you here to see Brent? I think he was scheduled to be out of the office this afternoon."

"I met with Brent over dinner last night. I am actually here to see you. Do you have time to talk?" Brent's dad asked, with a little gleam in his eye.

"For you, anything," Cora said as she followed him to Brent's office.

"You know, it wasn't that long ago that this was my office," Robert said, as he sat comfortably behind the desk in his old chair. "I miss it sometimes," he said wistfully, as he looked out the window.

"Mr. Locke," Cora began.

"Cora, we've been through this. Please call me Robert."

"Robert, what did you want to talk to me about?" Cora inquired. She was nervous. Maybe he somehow knew how much she cared for his son. She was racking her brain to think if she had done anything inappropriate at

The Del. He did see her and Brent in the spa. Maybe he wanted to talk to her about it.

"I want to start by saying that your performance at the conference was phenomenal. You are working way above the classification of an intern. I was so impressed with your talent that I contacted a few people I know. One of my friends, John Whitman, is looking for an Environmental Planner for his branch office in Santa Rosa. I told him about you and he would like you to fill the position at the start of the year. I spoke to Brent last night. Of course, he doesn't want to lose you, but he doesn't have a position like this to offer you. He wants you to stay, but he knows this is quite an opportunity for you. I have the terms and contract with me. Cora, I believe this is your destiny," Brent's dad said, enjoying the shocked look on Cora's face.

Cora was speechless. A promotion? It would be a huge step forward in her career. But she would have to leave Locke, Inc., Julie, her co-workers and Brent. Her head was spinning. What was it about Locke men that threw her life into utter chaos?

"Honestly, I don't know what to say. I'm very pleased and quite shocked," Cora finally managed to say.

"Can I assume that your answer is yes?"

"I'd be crazy to say no," Cora said, trying to get her face to show excitement and gratitude.

"Great! Here is the paperwork. I'm going to go call

John and tell him the good news," Robert said, as he squeezed Cora's shoulder.

"Thank you so much, Robert."

"The pleasure is all mine, Cora. All mine," Robert said, as he left the office.

Cora sat for a minute to collect herself. It was a great opportunity. She was nervous, but she knew in time, she would be comfortable in her new position. It wasn't like she could remain an intern forever. It was yet another step in the right direction for Cora. Seeing Brent at work was not helping her end her feelings for him. She needed physical distance to get him out of her mind.

Perhaps Brent's dad sensed her attraction for his son and that prompted him to move her out of the company. Or, more likely, Brent's mother pressured Robert to do it. She was pretty crafty and determined to move Cora out of the Brent's life. It didn't take long for Brent's mother to get her way. Regardless, she had just accepted a new position. The pay was incredible and the location was still within commute distance. She should have been brimming with joy. Instead, she focused on everything she would be losing. What really bothered her was that she would lose all the time she spent with Brent. It wasn't like they were friends and would see each other after she left. It would probably be one of the last times she sat in Brent's office. What had this man done to her? She was never this fragile when she dated other men and she wasn't even dating Brent.

The news of Cora leaving Locke, Inc. spread like wildfire. After calling her new boss, Brent's dad must have told Julie and Julie immediately found Cora. Everyone was excited for her and also sad to see her go. With the holidays approaching and Cora's planned trip to see her grandmother, it only left Cora with two weeks in her current position.

After a rather lonely weekend, Cora arrived a bit sluggish in the office on Monday. Everything was beginning to weigh on Cora: her break-up with Josh, starting a new job and leaving Brent and his company. When she returned to her desk after lunch, there was a large basket on her desk. The note on top of the basket read:

Cora,
Here are a few memories from our honeymoon in San Francisco.
I miss you.
Love Josh

Inside the basket were pictures from their fun day, bars of Ghirardelli chocolate, a crazy hat, cable car key chain, a ferry schedule, and a map of the city with the route of their day highlighted. Even though she tried to hold it back, a tear slipped down Cora's cheek. She headed toward the bathroom before anyone could see her. On her way, she kept her head down to avoid eye contact. In her attempt to remain hidden, she ran smack into Brent. The force of their collision knocked Cora to the ground. The tears she was holding back all came out. She was upset, hurt and terribly embarrassed.

She was a mess.

Brent leaned down and helped her up.
"Cora, are you ok? What's going on? You seem really upset," Brent said softly. He quickly glanced at his watch and asked, "Do you want to talk about it? Is there anything I can do to help you?"

"No, I don't want to keep you. I know you are busy," Cora said, trying to hide her red puffy eyes from Brent.

"I can see you are still upset. If you want to talk about this later, just let me know," Brent said softly.

"Thank you," Cora said as she walked over to the door. Cora was in no mood to talk, but it was nice that Brent showed concern. His soft words and tone soothed her. Cora returned to her desk and put the basket from Josh on the floor. She would deal with that later. Cora had work to do.

Chapter 10

Brent was out of the office the rest of the week, so it was pretty uneventful for Cora. She received one email from Brent on Thursday which read,

Corina,

Since we will be wine tasting, I hired a driver for the day, as I don't want to risk your safety by driving after a day in the Napa Valley. I will send a car to your residence. Please provide me with an address so I can notify the driving company. Thanks again for your assistance with this holiday project!

Brent

Cora was impressed with Brent's sensitivity toward her reputation and well-being. It was commendable that he looked out for his employees and thought about the image of his company. Cora quickly replied to Brent with her apartment address.

She practically counted the hours until she would be with Brent on Friday in Napa. Friday finally arrived, however, Cora woke up with mixed feelings about the day ahead. Although she couldn't wait to spend the day alone with Brent, she felt a little guilty about it. It was likely the last time she would be alone with him. The reality of this fact rocked her hard. She had grown attached to his presence in her life. He had a way of making her come alive; he challenged her unlike anyone she had ever met.

Cora paid special attention to getting ready for the day. She picked out some beige slacks, a classy long sleeve top and brown strappy sandals with a small heel. She debated if she should wear gold or silver jewelry. She finally decided on gold, as it accented her bronze skin and black hair. Her large gold hoops added a little sexiness to her outfit; she couldn't resist. Before she ran out the door, she sprayed some perfume on her wrist. She then checked her look in the mirror, gave herself a quick thumbs-up and put a smile on her face. If this was the last time she had alone with the man, she wanted him to remember her.

The driver picked her up at 9am, which left plenty of time to arrive at the Mondavi Winery and be on time to meet up with Brent. It was her first time visiting the Napa Valley region. Even though she lived in the Bay Area for years, she hadn't taken advantage of the opportunities to wine taste. In order to impress Brent, she did a little research on the winery's website the night before so she could get a lay of the land. Cora arrived promptly at 9:45am. She took a few minutes to reapply her makeup and check her phone for messages. After collecting herself, she walked inside the tasting room. The room was empty, so Cora took a seat by the window.

It was a very beautiful sunny California day, and while it was early December, it felt like a spring day in the Napa Valley. The harvest was over and the vines were full of yellow and brown leaves preparing themselves for winter. The rows and rows of vines spread across the fields and up into the rolling hills. The sun beamed through the withering leaves and splattered various patterns on the ground.

"How about this weather? Are you enjoying yourself, Corina? This is as good as it gets!" Brent said as he placed his hand on her shoulder.

The warmth of his touch quelled all of the morning's previous anxieties. She wasn't going to allow anything to interfere with their last few hours together, especially her own thoughts. Cora reached around and touched Brent's hand.

"Yes, I am already enjoying myself and thank you for asking me to assist you today," Cora said as she stood to face him.

"I usually do this holiday task by myself, but I thought a feminine touch would be nice this year."

"I am feminine," Cora said. She had no idea what she meant by the comment, but she said it with confidence.

Brent slowly looked her up and down and then replied, "I am glad you recognize that fact." He guided her over to the tasting bar.

"Brent, I don't think they are open until 10:00am," Cora said as she looked around the empty tasting room.

"They aren't. The Mondavi family and my parents are friends. My dad set us up with a private tasting today."

"THE Mondavi's?" Cora said, once again floored by the Locke family's connections.

"Yes, if you want to be formal about it. A staff member will be here at 11:00am for our tasting. I thought you might like a tour of the winery first. I have the keys to the buildings. Are you in?"

"I am in," Cora beamed.

"Let's go."

Brent led Cora on a tour throughout the entire vineyard. He showed her the barrels that stored the wine during fermentation, explained the various varieties of vines, described the history of the Mondavi family, and even showed her the famous cellar, which she knew nothing about.

"The Mondavi family is very supportive of the arts. They hold a summer concert series that is fabulous. They have been holding it for over 40 years. Have you come out for a concert before?" Brent asked.

"No. I read about it online. It sounds splendid," Cora said dreamily.

"It is pretty remarkable. They keep the concerts

relatively small so the gatherings are intimate. Before the concert, people arrive early and picnic on the grass. The concert is outside, so it adds a whole other dimension to the event."

"Do Grace and the kids like it?" Cora asked, trying to be polite. They were, after all, an extension of Brent and a huge part of his life.

"Yes. We all went to see the Colbie Caillat concert here this past summer, along with my dad and mother, of course. She was incredible."

Cora tried not to let her heart sink. It was easy to get caught up and forget the fact that he was unavailable. "That concludes our unofficial tour. Are you ready to get down to business?" Brent inquired as he opened the door to the tasting room for Cora.

"I sure am. So how many varieties do you want to include in each gift basket? How large are the baskets? Do you include other items? Are you purchasing for the southern offices as well?" Cora asked, as she stared at Brent in anticipation of his responses.

"Slow down there, tiger. Let me catch up to you. How about we taste first and we make decisions later?"

"Sorry, I am task oriented," Cora said with a sheepish smile on her face.

"I know, I like that about you."

"What else do you like?" Cora asked, as she playfully

batted her eyelashes.

"First of all, I like that you don't fish for compliments," Brent said teasingly.

Cora instantly turned red. She wanted to respond, but knew she would be playing right into Brent's hand. So instead, she played one of her best cards, the age-old tactic of diversion.

"It's a shame your father couldn't join us today. He is so friendly and full of life," Cora said in a slight attempt to get under Brent's skin.

"I heard he presented you with quite the offer the other day. He sure has taken a shine to you. My mother better watch out."

Cora laughed so hard, envisioning herself with Robert Locke. While he was charming, her heart already was lost to his son.

"It's a shame he isn't on the market. I might be interested, but I have a strict policy against dating married men," Cora said somewhat playfully, however, there was truth behind her statement.

"So, you flirt with them a little, but leave it at that?" Brent inquired as he brushed a few strands of hair out of Cora's face.

Cora laughed again. "I guess if I am being honest, I see no harm in innocent flirting."

"Actually, I am a little irritated with my father at the moment. He stole one of my best employees out from under my nose. What do you think of that?" Brent asked, as he raised his eyebrows.

"That is simply terrible. You need to have a talk with him. He must keep the best interest of the company in mind. How dare he interfere like that!" Cora said, failing at her attempt to keep a straight face.

"We shared a few words already, but I wouldn't want to bore you with the details."

"Oh, it wouldn't bore me," Cora said eagerly.

"No. No. We have work to do here. And just on cue, here is the lovely lady that is going to assist us with our tasting lesson," Brent said, as a beautiful redhead walked into the tasting room and introduced herself.

"Hi. My name is Audrey. I am here to host your private tasting. I understand you are friends of the family and I have been asked to give you very special treatment. We have some private reserves for you to taste today. Follow me and we will go back into the private tasting room."

Cora wasn't sure whom they needed privacy from, as the tasting room was empty. She saw cars in the parking lot and was beginning to wonder if people were being diverted to another area on purpose.

When they entered the private room, Cora couldn't believe the ambiance. There was a nice fire crackling in the fireplace, the windows looked out over the vineyards, a portrait of Robert Mondavi hung above the mantel, two couches and a large antique chair were set near the fire, a Persian rug was on the floor, and flowers were placed all over the room. Off to one corner was a table set up with an exquisite lunch, more flowers and numerous wine glasses.

"Would you like to sit at the table or by the fire for the tasting?" Audrey asked Brent.

"The fire, please," Brent said as he turned his head in Cora's direction to gauge her response.

"That would be lovely," Cora said as she walked over to the couch. Cora was surprised that Brent consulted with her.

Audrey grabbed a few bottles of wine and sat in the chair by the couches. Cora was happy to be right next to Brent on the couch. She was close enough to feel his breath on her neck. She tried to pay attention to Audrey, but it was nearly impossible with Brent so close.

"Today, you are going to taste our Cabernet Sauvignon, Fume Blanc, Chardonnay, Pinot Noir and Merlot. As I mentioned before, these are the family's private reserves. We take these from our best years. After I am finished with my presentation, I will leave them over on the table for you to enjoy," Audrey said as she delved into her presentation on the various types of wine.

Brent was attentive, but Cora was surely not focused on the discussion of wine. Brent's arm lingered on top of the couch close to Cora's shoulder. She could feel his presence and it drove her completely wild. He oozed a masculine energy that ignited every part of Cora's being. She had never felt such attraction. It was intoxicating. It felt so good to want someone so bad. She was alive and never in her life would she be dead again. She was awakened.

"That concludes my talk. If you have any questions, I will be in the other room," Audrey said as she left the room.

Brent turned to Cora, "Are you well-versed in all the varieties of the wines?"

Cora panicked. She was so busy thinking about Brent that she didn't hear one word Audrey said. "Sorry, I hope I am better at tasting than listening today," Cora responded.

"Let's test that theory. Grab a glass and let's get this tasting party started," Brent said as he took the cork off the first bottle.

"Okay. We have tasted all of them. Which is your favorite?" Brent asked as he put the cork on the last bottle.

"I have no idea. I can't even remember which one I have in this glass," Cora replied, completely confused.

"Some help you have been. Let's try a different

approach, are there any you didn't like?"

"Really?" Cora said, as she teasingly punched Brent's arm.

"We are getting nowhere fast, Corina."

"Are we supposed to get somewhere?" Cora asked, concerned that they needed to be at another winery. She was having so much fun here.

"No need to panic. It is fun to see you so relaxed. Wine can be a truth serum."

"It sure is, Mr. Locke. Ask me anything and I will tell you the answer," Cora said, all brave and sure of herself.

"Have you determined if you are in love with Josh?" Brent said very seriously as he stared at her.

"No. I don't think I am," Cora said, not breaking his stare.

"When will you know for sure?"

Cora busted up. Brent was so calculated, precise and focused. "I don't know. I am hoping this trip to my grandmother's will help me sort it all out. I broke up with him on the way home from Montana. I just couldn't see myself living out there. I love the Bay Area. It is a part of me and I don't want to be anywhere else."

"Is that why you were crying the other day?" Brent asked tenderly.

"Yes. It was part of the reason," Cora said very quietly.

"What else caused you to be upset?"

"It is too embarrassing to admit."

"You can tell me anything, Corina." Brent said as he put his hand in hers.

"Truthfully, there is a large part of me that doesn't want to leave the company. I've grown so attached to everyone. It is like family."

"I know the feeling. I don't want you to go, either," Brent said as he leaned close to her. The tip of his nose brushed against hers. Cora looked up and stared directly into his eyes then she closed them in sweet anticipation.

"I am sorry to interrupt. The rest of your lunch has arrived. I will put it over here on the table," Audrey said as she quickly exited the room.

"Let's get some food in your stomach to go with that wine we just tasted," Brent said as he helped Cora off the couch. Cora wasn't sure, but she thought they were just about to kiss. Or was she just imagining it all? The wine was slightly clouding her judgment.

As they settled into their seats, they talked, really talked. Barriers did not exist. All topics were available.

Expression without judgment was their guiding principle for their communication. As they moved from topic to topic, Cora was continually amazed at the ease of being with him. She did not have to pretend to be something she was not. She was truly herself and that was okay. With Brent, she saw her own potential being reflected back to her. Life was clearer with him by her side. She was feeling limitless, beautiful, and secure. After they finished their meal, Cora was ready for the conversation to go deeper and more personal.

"Tell me something about you," Cora said as she traced the top of her glass with her finger.

"What do you want to know?"

"I want to know what drives you," Cora stated, intently focused on him.

"What drives me? Let's see. That is a very interesting question. My life has changed a lot over the last few years."

"Since you took over the company?" Cora asked.

"Yes and no. Everything changed about a year ago when my brother, Derek, told us he had pancreatic cancer. It was quite a shock to everyone. Of course, we rallied around him and gave him our complete support. The whole experience made me stop and look at my life. I reprioritized things and started to live more. Does that make sense?"

"Yes. It does," Cora softly said.

"He went through intensive treatment and for awhile it looked promising. Then more test results came back and the cancer had spread throughout his entire body. It was already at stage four and there wasn't much the doctors could do for him. We tried all the Eastern practices. We brought in healers from all over the world. That is when my dad took leave from the company. So in the middle of this family crisis, I began acting as the CEO. It was a real difficult time in my life. Five months later, my brother died. Part of me died that day too. It was an awful time for me. After his death, my dad retired. He couldn't take the day-to-day anymore and he walked away from life for a few months. When he was talking with you at the company dinner at The Del, it was the first time I have seen him laugh in some time."

"When my dad disconnected, I had to stand up and lead the family and the company. It wasn't easy, and quite honestly, I don't know how I made it through. My mom was a complete mess. She is so used to controlling everything in her world and here she had no control over anything. Grace and the kids were totally lost. I had to be strong. I was left with no other choice. So I was strong. I became pretty robotic. I didn't let any emotions into my life. I was afraid if I let myself feel anything, I would fall completely apart."

"And, I just miss my brother so much. We were very close and he is always on my mind. I can feel his spirit at times and I just linger in those moments as long as possible. I never knew that love and loss could cause such deep emotions. The answer to my pain has been to close myself off to everyone around me. In fact, this is the first time I have even discussed my brother's death with anyone," Brent said before he got extremely quiet.

Cora stood up from her seat and moved over to Brent. She put her arms around him and pulled him close. Cora didn't know what to do. She just continued to hold him close and whisper soft encouragements into his ear. Her heart broke for the man of steel she held in her arms. Even in his pain, he was still strong. After a few minutes, Brent stood and returned Cora's embrace.

"Corina, there is something about you that just opens me," Brent said as he held her chin in his hand.

Before she knew it, his soft lips were on hers. She responded to his kiss and ran her hand through his hair. She was past caring. She wanted this more than anything she had ever wanted before. His tongue tantalized her and sent shock waves throughout her body from the top of head down to her toes. He gently tugged the back of her hair. He took her hand and strongly pulled her close to his side. Her waist was near him, so she pushed herself close to Brent's body. She could feel the shape of his body and his warmth next to hers: the outline of his ribs, the curve of his hips, and the muscles in his arms. They all beckoned to be touched and caressed. His masculine shape sent shivers of desire right to her heart. She wanted him. Her body knew he could bring her pleasure and it yearned deeply for that feeling, that rush of emotion. The sparks of passion ignited secret parts of her that only he seemed to know existed.

"Cora, it feels so good to touch you," Brent murmured seductively in Cora's ear. "If there weren't people right outside that door," Brent started to say, as a knock at the door interrupted him.

Audrey stuck her head in the door and said, "Hi again. Our reception desk received a call from your mother, Brent. She has been attempting to reach you on your cell phone, but she says it goes right to voicemail. She asked that I deliver the message promptly," Audrey said with an emphasis on the word 'promptly'.

"Thank you, Audrey," Brent said with a wry smile as Audrey closed the door.

"I sure hope everything is alright with your family," Cora said as she turned away from Brent. The mere mention of Brent's mother caused Cora to snap back to reality. Before Cora could walk away, Brent took her hand.

"Corina, don't let my mother scare you. Ever since my brother died, she has been a little overprotective of me. She was heartbroken when Derek died. I do my best to appease her worrying nature as much as possible."

"You are a good son, Brent."

"Thank you," Brent said.

Cora stood next to the window taking in the view. Off in the distance she saw a man, woman and child playing by a large oak tree. Why wasn't Grace helping Brent with the choosing of the wines? Were there problems in their marriage? Was Brent closing off Grace due to the passing of his brother? They appeared quite happy when Cora saw them together at The Del. And, most curiously, she wondered why Brent shared his very personal feelings for the very first time on losing his brother to her and not Grace?

Thinking about Grace brought Cora back to the dreaded reality and questioning of how this affair could go any further with Brent. While she was having a wonderful time with him, she needed to keep herself in check. It was just so difficult whenever he came near her. She vowed to be strong.

"Lost in your thoughts, Corina" Brent asked as he came up from behind.

"I was just thinking about you kissing me," Cora admitted. What she really was thinking was how much she wanted to not to stop with the kissing. She wanted to go all the way with him.

Assuming Cora was having conscience problems, Brent said, "I want to apologize for my behavior if I made you uncomfortable by moving too fast. Also, you still have a week left with the company and then I will no longer be your CEO and we won't have to worry about any gossip. Please forgive me."

Not quite sure of the full meaning of what he just said and not wanting to spoil the day by asking him any clarifying questions, especially that part about not having to worry about any gossip in a week, Cora smiled saying "Brent, no apologies are needed, as I loved every minute of that kiss. Actually, I was thinking if I am wrong, I don't want to be right. But, we are in a public place," was the best Cora could muster, adding, "And, I would not want to cause you any embarrassment."

Brent and his quick wit shot back with, "Your hair could cause us some embarrassment for sure! Do you want to borrow my comb?"

"I do have a brush. Does it really look that bad?" Cora asked as she walked over to a mirror. It looked like a rat had been building a nest in it.

Oh my, it sure does, she thought to herself as she brushed her hair. They were both all smiles as Brent stood behind her and gazed in the mirror. They looked good together.

"Are you enjoying yourself, Corina? I actually had something else in mind if you are interested."

"Of course. What do you want to do?" Cora asked, hoping it involved being near Brent.

"Come with me," Brent said as he grabbed Cora's hand. Cora obeyed. She would have gone anywhere with Brent.

Brent opened the car door for Cora and provided the driver with directions as they comfortably settled side by side in the back seat. He took control of every situation in such a perfect manner. Cora was glad, since she was still wobbly from the effects of Brent's touch. She was so enamored with him that she couldn't tell if she was coming or going. It was such a new experience for her to be so drawn into someone's presence.

They headed north up Highway 29 toward Calistoga. Each vineyard they passed grew even more beautiful than the last. The grass was green from the recent rains. The vines exposed a few leaves, but mostly branches. The sky was blue. The clouds were a bright white. The beauty was simple and distinct, yet almost unbearable.

Cora could feel the intensity of all of the sensations hitting her at once. She wanted to capture it all so she could relive the moment over and over again.
Brent's hand was near Cora's leg, which excited her. She wasn't sure how much longer she would be able to restrain herself. Cora was watching Brent out of the corner of her eye. She caught him staring at her breasts and she gained a secret pleasure from his interest. She sat up straighter to give him a better look. Her blouse was slightly disheveled so one side exposed the edge of her lacy bra. Desire coursed throughout her body. Brent had merely given her a taste of what she was sure would be the most satisfying sexual experience any woman could ever want. Grace was a very lucky woman.

"What are you thinking right now, Cora? You have a smirk on your face that can only mean that you are brewing up some trouble," Brent said as he squeezed her leg.

"Me? Trouble? Never. I was just thinking about you," Cora vaguely responded.

"What about me?"

"I was thinking about how you were just looking at my chest," Cora said as she looked Brent straight in the eye.

"You caught me. I won't deny it," Brent said, returning Cora's powerful gaze.

They had arrived near Calistoga at The Sterling Vineyards. The winery sat high upon a hill that overlooked the Napa Valley. The stucco buildings were white and the entire scene held the feel of an exclusive monastery.

"Are you sure this isn't a convent?" Cora asked as she peered at the spectacular buildings off in the distance.

"Why? Are you thinking of joining a convent? Before you take your vows, I think we should make sure you really want to live the celibate lifestyle," Brent said, sending Cora a knowing glance.

"I'm not that bad," Cora said as her lower lip protruded out for effect.

"I know you aren't that fragile, Corina. I've seen you take on some pretty tough people and hold your own."

"Like who?" Cora asked, puzzled by his comment.

"Well, my mother, for one. She isn't the warmest person when you first meet her," Brent said as he ran his hand through Cora's hair. It was challenging for Cora to concentrate when Brent's hands were on her. Not that she was complaining one single bit.

"Yes, your mother is a bit direct."

Brent threw his head back in a fit of laughter. "She would take that as a compliment! So, should we check out the convent?"

"I would love to, but do we have to walk all the way up there? It looks like quite a strenuous climb from down here," Cora said as she looked down at her heels.

"Cora, you have quite the imagination. We aren't walking. We will take the aerial tram to the top of the winery," Brent said as they walked over to a building.

If Cora had been paying more attention to the things around her, she would have noticed the large cables suspended high in the air. After she noticed the cables, she saw a series of small trams ascending and descending from the winery. It looked so European. Brent purchased tickets and they went to the platform to enter the gondola car. Brent sat on one side and Cora sat on the other facing each other in order to balance out the weight. Cora would have preferred to sit in Brent's lap, but she held back and attempted to demonstrate some restraint. Luckily, Cora was not afraid of heights. In fact, she enjoyed being as high as possible since the views were dramatic. The little ski-like tram moved progressively up the hillside and offered them an extraordinary view of the grape fields, trees, pond and surrounding mountains as well as the sounds of the silence that comes with being high in the air above the trees.

It was late afternoon and the sun was starting to set. The day's dwindling light cast an assortment of beautiful colorful shades and shadows all across the Napa Valley. Cora loved sunsets and was feeling ecstatic; she couldn't remember a time in her life that she felt more content and confident. She was living in the moment and felt at peace. Love. Life. It was all so much richer now, all because of the man at her side. Yes, she was responsible for her own thoughts and actions. However, when she was with him, she felt a shift, everything settled inside her and she was wide open to experience the beauty of everyone and everything they encountered.

Brent reached over and skimmed the back of his hand gently across her face. He took her face in both of his hands and affectionately pressed his lips upon hers.

"Beautiful," Brent affectionately said.

"I know. I can't get over the view."

"I am referring to the woman with me. Everyone she passes enjoys her outward beauty, yet her inner beauty is reserved for those who have the privilege of knowing her. I want to know her even more. Do you think she will let me in?" Brent asked with such sincerity.

"Yes," Cora answered. "I want to know you too.

There is a mysterious quality that completely surrounds you. You are the most capable man I know."

"Capable?" Brent questioned as he raised his eyebrows.

"That didn't come out right," Cora laughed, as her cheeks flushed. "When I spend time with you, I know you will take care of everything. I can be myself when I am with you. Does that make any sense?"

Brent smiled. "Cora, you have the sweetest spirit. Thank you for sharing it with me."

They had arrived at the end of the ride. They exited the tram and made their way to the first tasting area. Cora was so caught up in the atmosphere that she paid no attention to the server and his description of the wine. Honestly, it all tasted good. She enjoyed all of the fancy varieties: Port, Cabernet, Chardonnay, Pinot Noir and more. It didn't take long for the wine to weave its magic upon her again. Brent placed her hand in his and guided her on the rest of the tour.

The history of the winery was described throughout the self-guided tour. Cora enjoyed reading about how the winery was modeled after the Greek island of Mykonos. Now she understood the inspiration for the Mediterranean-style architecture. They walked out to a large terrace that offered them a spectacular view. The historic church bells greeted them and rang out in a glorious melody. All Cora could do was smile.

"Shall we continue the tour? The view from the top at sunset is a must-see," Brent said as he hooked his arm in Cora's.

"Most definitely!" Cora stated with enthusiasm.

Cora and Brent walked up a few set of stairs to enter the main tasting room. "Are you enjoying yourself, Cora?"

"You know I am, Brent," Cora said as she put her hand in his pocket.

"Looking for something?" Brent questioned.

Cora fumbled for a response. She had no idea that she had stuck her hand in his pocket. "How embarrassing! I think you might have to cut me off," Cora said.

"We will have some dinner after this last tasting and don't worry, what happens today stays in Napa," Brent promised as he grinned and nudged his elbow into her ribs.

They concluded their quick tour and walked down a short hill for their return trip on the tramway. The sun was almost down and the scene before them was again breathtaking. They stood in silence at a lookout point to soak in the beauty of the day and the view of the valley. The ride down was quieter than the ride up. It was a time of reflection for both of them. A lot had transpired during the day's events. Brent walked Cora over to the car, but did not open the door. Instead he opened the trunk and pulled out two blankets and a large picnic basket.

"Let's go stake out a spot on the lawn by the pond," Brent said as he led Cora over to the water.

Two ducks were busy swimming around the pond, trying their best to avoid the spray from the fountain. One duck was a mallard. He shamelessly pursued the female until she was too tired to swim away from him. Or maybe it was her plan all along to play hard-to-get. Brent laid out one of the blankets and set down the picnic basket. Cora found a spot on the blanket and took off her shoes. Brent opened the basket. He set out lemonade, crackers, a plate of cheese and a can of mixed nuts. Cora was happy to see the food.

"Are you cold?" Brent asked.

"Not yet. Thank you."

"Just let me know and we can cover up with the other blanket. Of course, I am going to watch both of your hands under the blanket. Next thing you know, you'll be into my wallet," Brent said jokingly.

"Funny," Cora giggled.

When the sun vanished behind the mountain and took all trace of itself with it, the stars began to shine against the darkening sky. The full moon provided the mood lighting as Brent lit a candle he had in the basket.

"You could offer a lot of men lessons on romance. I cannot get over the lengths you have gone to prepare such an enchanting day. You simply amaze me, Mr. Locke."

"I've wanted to spend some special time with you before you left the company, Corina. You have fascinated me ever since the day I found you in my office pawing at my things," Brent said chuckling.

"Pawing? Really?" Cora said as she threw a dried leaf at Brent.

"Who knows what may have happened if I didn't come in at that time? Perhaps you would have pocketed my picture? One can never be too cautious with strangers."

Cora leaned over Brent and wrestled him to the ground. Her thoughts of being strong today were forgotten for the moment. "Perhaps you are right. Or maybe I would have riffled through your desk and stolen all of the company's secrets? Did you ever think of that?"

"No, I can't say that I did. You are a clever woman. Do you really think your small body will keep me pinned down?"

"It has worked so far," Cora said, once again proud of her accomplishment.

"It's only because I like the feel of you on top of me."

"I am still winning you!" Cora announced.

"Not for long, Cora. Not for long," Brent said as he moved quickly and pinned her to the ground.

"Now who is winning?" Brent asked boldly.

"I am still winning."

"No, you aren't. I am on top of you now, Cora."

"I know. That means I am still winning you. It is what I wanted in the first place. I wanted to feel you on top of me, the shape of your muscles and the bulge in your pants. I win," Cora said as she softly placed her lips on Brent's mouth. Brent was too stunned to deny her the pleasure. He grabbed the blanket and placed it on top of them. He didn't want her sweet body to feel the chill of the night air. Cora basked in the satisfaction of it all. It was pure bliss.

The evening continued with more conversation and laughter. However, the back and forth banter returned to provide them a safety net from the inevitable. Neither was completely aware that deep down they were fighting a losing battle by trying to restrain themselves from their intense mutual attraction. Brent continued to pull out delicious items to share from the picnic basket. Cora clapped her hands like a little girl when he brought out a slice of cheesecake.

"I guessed correctly. I remembered that you are a chocolate snob, so I didn't want to have the wrong piece of chocolate cake. Cheesecake seemed the safest bet," Brent said proudly.

"Great idea!" Cora said before she drove her fork into the creamy dessert.

"I have some coffee in a thermos if you want some," Brent asked.

"Please," Cora said between bites.

"Don't worry. I am not having any cheesecake. You don't have to eat it so fast."
Cora took her fork and playfully jabbed Brent. "You are quite the funny man, aren't you?"

"I sure am. You just wait," Brent replied with a stern look on his face. Cora was slightly concerned if someday she would be able to handle all of the pleasure a man like Brent could bring her.

About an hour after the coffee was gone, Brent and Cora packed up the picnic basket and folded the blankets. They made their way to the car by the soft moonlight. Side-by-side they walked. When they got in the car, Brent's phone vibrated. He peered down at it. "Wow, I have 23 missed calls. Want to bet they are all from my mother?"

"Goodness, I forgot about her. Didn't she want you to call her earlier?"

"She sure did. I will be sure to get back to her tomorrow," Brent said as he put his phone down. Cora was positive that Brent's decisive stubborn side came from his mother. In many ways, they were alike. Yet over the last few months, Cora observed Brent's soft, tender side that was so much like his father. Brent was a perfect combination of both of his parents.

The drive back to the Mondavi Winery was pleasant. Cora replayed countless scenes in her head from the incredible day. She was going to write it all down when she got to her apartment so she would never forget.

"Cora, thank you for spending the day with me."

"No, thank you. I can't remember the last time I have ever had so much fun. Thank you for all of the work you put into planning today. It is a day I will never forget, Brent."

"You are welcome. Will you be coming to the company Christmas party tomorrow night?"

"I can hardly wait!" Cora said already mentally picking out her outfit.

"Remember what happens in Napa, stays in Napa," Brent declared.

"I agree," Cora said completely forgetting about the office dynamics. It was a good thing she only had one week of work left at Locke, Inc.

"I will call you tomorrow morning," Brent said as he hugged Cora.

"I would like that a lot," Cora said, as he opened the door for door and tipped the driver with instructions to get her home safe and sound.

Brent waved as Cora was driving off. Cora knew it was silly, but she already missed him. She didn't want to ask him where he was going, since she knew it was surely home to his wife and family. Cora couldn't bear to think about all of that now. She knew she could never have a relationship with Brent, but she just wanted this one perfect day with him to be forever in her heart. She had never known a man like Brent Locke. For a man like him to be attracted to her blew Cora's mind. She was surely the luckiest woman alive, at least for that day. It was more than a dream come true.

During her ride home, she kept replaying the day over and over: the moment Brent first kissed her, the feeling of him sitting near her, the continuous laugher and his fingers in her hair. Cora's cheeks hurt from the immense smile plastered to her face.

When Cora arrived home, she attempted to get some sleep. Her body was tired, but she was still emotionally charged. She wanted to share her excitement with someone, but she wasn't willing to be judged. After lying in bed for over an hour without sleeping, she got up and checked her email. There were five new messages from Josh. She felt bad ignoring them, however, it also wasn't fair to string him along. Cora was thrilled when she then saw a message from Brent. She quickly opened it:

Hi Corina,

I want you to know how much I enjoy being with such a sweet and smart spirit as you. Thank you for allowing me to personally confide in you today. You made me feel so comfortable. Thanks for a great day!

BTW – Thanks also for the difficult wine selections that had to be made today!

☺
Brent

Cora was so touched by Brent's email. He had a romantic side, which surprised her. The more she learned about him, the more mysterious he became. It was deliciously wonderful that there were multiple facets to his personality.

Cora quickly replied to his email:

Hi Brent,

Thank you for today's precious gift of getting to know you better! You are a remarkable man. Your selfless generosity toward me has meant so much. I look forward to seeing you tomorrow.

Cora

After sending her message, Cora fell fast asleep. She didn't need to fantasize about him that evening since the reality of her day far surpassed any fantasy she could create.

Chapter 11

Cora woke up early on Saturday. It was already the middle of December. In just one week, she would be flying out to New York to visit her grandmother. Her employment with Locke Inc. would be over. She decided to put that all aside and focus on the day ahead. She had a million and one things to do to prepare for the Christmas party later in the evening. Her first order of business was to go buy a sexy dress. Somehow after spending the previous day with Brent, her black cocktail dress was no longer fit for the occasion. She wanted Brent to drool when he saw her. Cora made a hair appointment for a cut and style. If she had time, she was going to spring for a manicure and a pedicure. Cora was very happy. Spring was welling inside of her and she couldn't contain the joy.

Cora dragged her roommate Lynn along on her shopping adventure. Lynn couldn't understand why Cora was so excited about a company party.

"Remind me again why you aren't taking Josh along as your date?" Lynn repeatedly inquired.

"Hello? We broke up. It's over. Why is this so difficult for you to comprehend?" Cora said, slightly irritated that Lynn kept bringing it up.

"I just don't understand why you broke up with him. The man is handsome, kind and completely in love with you. He is heartbroken."

"Lynn! We've been through this already," Cora said yet again.

"I know. I just feel for the guy. And now that his mom is sick."

"His mom is sick? How do you know?" Cora was concerned. She genuinely cared for Josh's mom.

"Well, Josh comes by every once in a while to talk. He misses you a lot. He lost his girlfriend and best friend all in one day."

Cora knew how he felt. As much as she didn't want to admit it, she really missed talking to Josh. She just thought it was a cleaner break to stop all communication. Truth be told, she wasn't sure if she trusted herself around Josh and she didn't want to fall back into a comfortable pattern.

"What's going on with his mom?" Cora asked quietly.

"She was just diagnosed with breast cancer. It looks like the doctor caught it in time. Of course, Josh is very worried. He's headed back home Monday to spend the holidays with his family. I think it will be good for him to be surrounded by his loved ones. He's taken the break-up pretty hard," Lynn said.

"I feel terrible. I just don't know what I can do for Josh," Cora said as a tear slipped down her cheek. "I never wanted to hurt him.

Lynn wrapped her arms around Cora. "I know. The whole situation just sucks. Come on; let's focus on our mission to find you a sizzling dress."

Cora and Lynn had a blast scouring the stores for the perfect dress. Cora could not bring herself to come to a decision. Lynn finally had to step in and she picked a sassy red dress for Cora to buy. They found some hot black heels and then made their way over to the salon. They both indulged in manis and pedis right before Cora's hair appointment. Cora chose a brilliant red nail polish to match her dress. The polish was called Siren Red, which fit Cora's mood perfectly. The stylist curled all of Cora's black tresses, which took forever. Cora barely recognized herself when the stylist was finished. She was simply gorgeous.

When they got home, Lynn helped Cora with her make-up and jewelry. Cora was like a giddy schoolgirl by the time she left. The party was in a posh restaurant in Sausalito. Cora couldn't wait to see Brent's expression when he got a look at her.

The drive to Sausalito was a breeze since there was no traffic. Nerves got a hold of her when she arrived at the restaurant, but she threw them aside. She looked and felt incredible.

When Cora walked into the room where the party was

being held, things were already in full swing. A live band was warming up. Everyone was all dressed up and having a wonderful time. Cora felt Brent's stare long before she could locate him in the crowd. When her eyes found his, a sly smile of recognition crossed his face. He kept eye contact as he moved toward her and stood only inches away.

"Corina, you look stunning."

"Thank you, Brent. I picked out this dress for you."

"And the nail polish?" Brent asked as he nodded toward her hands and feet.

"Yes, the polish too," Cora said, embarrassed that she admitted primping for him. She didn't want to come across as desperate.

"I want to show you something. Follow me," Brent said as he took off. Cora followed him over to a table full of cases of Mondavi wine.

"What is this?" Cora inquired.

"The wine we selected for the employees," Brent said.

"I can see that much. When did you manage to pick it out?"

"After you told me yesterday how much you enjoyed the Cabernet Sauvignon, I ordered cases of it."

"You ordered my favorite wine," Cora said touched by

his gesture.

"Remember? Our mission yesterday was to order wine as part of the Christmas bonus?" Brent said as he elbowed Cora in the ribs.

"Yes, I remember. I am just piecing it all together."

"Are you impressed?" Brent asked, raising one eyebrow.

"Yes, I am impressed," Cora said, giving into Brent's need for affirmation.

"You just wait," Brent said before he wandered off to mingle with the other staff.

Cora found Julie and some other women sitting at a table and joined them. The party was in full swing and getting louder and louder. Cora didn't say much and preferred watching Brent instead. She enjoyed listening to the cattiness of the women. She felt like a chicken in the hen house. It was pretty funny.

"As always, Brent is quite striking tonight," one of Cora's co-workers said. "I can't believe my boss is so hot."

"I think he looks exceptionally happy. He keeps looking over here. I wonder if his ears are burning from us talking about him," another co-worker cackled.

The conversation blurred for Cora when she saw Grace. Cora completely overlooked the fact that Grace could be in attendance. Other staff had brought their spouses, why would Brent leave his at home? After all, he was the host of the event. Grace wore a floor length beige dress that clung to her well-proportioned body. Her long gloves added a touch of elegance that reminded Cora of Grace Kelly. The diamonds at her ears and throat occasionally caught the light and shimmered across the room.

Grace was standing with Brent's mother, another unwelcome surprise. Cora rose to make an escape. Suddenly, she felt a tug on her arm.

"Cora, sweetheart, I have been sent to fetch you. My wife wants to congratulate you on your new job," Robert Locke said as he swiftly guided Cora to Brent's mother and Grace. The ladies were locked in a lively conversation when Cora unhappily arrived.

Robert interrupted them, "Darling, I found her."

Brent's mother did not look very enthused. A tight smile crossed her face.

"Robert tells me you have only one week left. I was very happy to hear the news," Brent's mother sardonically said to Cora.

"Thank you," Cora stiffly said. She was extremely uncomfortable.

"I don't think we have officially met. I am Grace Locke. It is such a pleasure to meet you. Brent has tried to introduce us several times at the conference in

San Diego, but it never seemed to work out," Grace said as she shook Cora's hand. Cora could smell her sweet perfume and was taken by her kind smile. Grace carried an aura of calming strength that drew Cora to her. It was difficult to hate her. Cora could see the lump of a large ring under her glove on her left hand. It tore at Cora's heart.

"Robert and Brent talk about you nonstop. I was beginning to wonder if you existed or were just an illusion," Grace said as she touched her hand to Cora's shoulder and drew in to whisper to Cora. "Robert also said that you were quite beautiful. He loves women with long dark hair. Keep your eye on that one," Grace said as she drew back and winked at Cora. Cora couldn't believe what she just heard when Brent approached the group.

"What am I missing out on?" interjected Brent.

Just as these words were coming out of his mouth, his mother moved right and in put her arm around Brent for an interrogation. "Brent, why didn't you return my call yesterday? I was worried when I couldn't reach you. Didn't the Mondavi staff deliver my message to you? Is your phone broken?" Brent's mother said.

Amazingly, she actually spoke a little softer to him than Cora anticipated.

"Mother, I was wrapped up in a very important engagement yesterday, so I turned off my phone. Plus, I knew I would see you this evening," Brent said sternly. There was a little tension in the air.

Grace moved over and hugged Brent. "The wine selection this year is perfect. Did you see any of the family?"

"I am glad you approve of my choice. Sorry to say none of the Mondavi's was at the vineyard yesterday, but the assistance and treatment I received was special," Brent said as he smiled at Cora.

The band changed gears and switched to a slow number. Grace grabbed Brent's hand and led him to the dance floor. Robert turned to Cora, "May I have this dance?"

Cora obliged, "Of course."

She just wanted to be far away from Brent's mother. They danced right next to Brent and Grace. His mother was right; Brent and Grace made a handsome couple. Cora caught snippets of their conversation. Each time she heard their combined laughter, her heart sank a little more. What was she doing? They were married. What would she be left with – more heartache?

After the song ended, Cora thanked Robert and sat back down at the table. The women were still talking about Brent and now Grace was the new topic.

"In my opinion, it is unfair to the rest of the ladies that Grace Locke is so incredibly attractive. How are we ever supposed to land a man like Brent with women like that snatching them all up?" one of the women said.

"I hear you, but she is really nice, which makes it even worse," another replied.

The more Cora watched Grace and Brent swirl around the dance floor, the worse she felt. When she could take no more, she went outside to get some air. It was peaceful and the moon was full. Cora was so uncomfortable that she made an agreement with herself to stay outside for awhile, then go inside and make one last appearance and quietly depart. She had been caught up in a fantasy with Brent just one day earlier, but the cold harsh reality slammed itself in her face. Brent belonged to Grace and not Cora. But why didn't he take Grace to Mondavi to select the company wines, a voice in her head asked.

"Keeping the moon company?" Brent said, as he stood next to Cora on the deck of the restaurant.

"Sometimes I need to just break away from reality," Cora said.

"I like that about you. You walk on your own individual path, unfazed by the norms of society," Brent said as he edged closer to Cora. His hands brushed against her hips and rubbed against her panties.

"Are you sure you should do that? Someone might see us," Cora said as her body began to betray her resolve to stay away from him. She knew she should just walk away, but her feet refused to move. She knew she should tell him to stop, but she remained silent.

"Walk with me," replied Brent, assuming control.

"Does anyone ever tell you, no?" Cora inquired.

"Not often," Brent said as they walked through the parking lot and through the streets of Sausalito.

Neither spoke as they made their way down to the bay. When they reached the water's edge, Brent leaned down and kissed Cora. The passion surged through them. She immediately responded to his touch and met him with hers. She drew him close and rubbed herself against him.

"Corina, I want you," Brent rasped against Cora's face.

The slight evening stubble on his face added a masculine sensation to the already intense passion.

"I want you too, but am afraid," Cora answered.

"I want this to be right and with integrity," Brent said as he ran his hand through her hair. "I need to return to the party. My family is there and I have obligations."

"Ok," Cora said disappointed that reality returned so quickly.

"We should be careful," Brent reminded her.

"Ok, there is no need to explain," Cora replied as she fixed a forced smile on her face. She was not sure what he was talking about with the integrity and being careful stuff – but she knew she did not feel encouraged or claimed by him so all could say was, "Brent, let's just go back to the party."

They walked back to the restaurant. When Brent entered the room, Cora slipped over to the ladies room. As she walked away, she heard his voice through an amplified microphone thanking all the Locke employees for a very successful year. She could no longer hear him when she entered the restroom. Cora was glad that she didn't have to see him standing next to Grace. It was all too difficult for her to swallow. She had to get out of there.

On her way out the door, Julie shoved three bottles of wine at her. Cora took them to avoid having a discussion. The beverages only served as a reminder of what would never be. She put them in the back of her car and drove off into the now rainy night.

By the time she made it home, her anger had turned into another pity party. Feeling depressed, she carried the wine in her arms and walked to her front door. The door was unlocked as she entered. Josh was sitting at the kitchen table with Lynn. Cora froze.

"Cora, I didn't expect you home so soon," Lynn apologized as she grabbed her car keys and walked out of the apartment, leaving Josh and Cora alone.

"I didn't mean to startle you. I can leave," Josh said as he hung his head.

"It's fine. I was just about to open of these very fine

bottles of Napa wine and drink it through a straw. I had a rough evening," Cora said in a feeling sorry for herself tone, as she searched for a corkscrew.

"Do you want to talk about it?"

"No, I just want to forget the whole night," Cora said as she finally located an opener.

"Let me help you," Josh said as he took the bottle from Cora.

He poured two glasses and took them over to the couch.

"Lynn told me about your mom. I was really sorry to hear the news. How is she doing?"

"She is the strongest one out of all of us. You remind me so much of her," Josh said as he looked tenderly at Cora.

They fell quickly back into the rhythm of conversation as they sipped the wine. Cora was feeling mellow now. She had missed dinner when Brent and she were out walking. Before she knew what happened, Josh was kissing her. It felt so foreign to her lips after just kissing Brent only hours before. She wasn't completely into it, but her frustration about Brent encouraged her to return Josh's kiss. When he reached for her breast, his hand felt odd. While she knew this man touching her, there was no passion or spark. It confused Cora. She wanted desperately to feel for Josh what she felt for Brent, but it wasn't there.

Instead of pressing Josh away, she closed her eyes and once again found herself pretending that it was Brent caressing her. The passion began to ignite within her. It was Brent taking off her dress. It was Brent laying her down on the floor. It was Brent removing her panties. It was Brent pressing his body on tops of hers. She wanted Brent to take her; to make her his.

"Cora, I love you." Josh's voice shook Cora out of her fantasy. It was Josh that was about to enter her. The shock of it all rocked her to the core.

"What's wrong?" Josh asked when he saw the expression on her face.

"I'm not ready for this," Cora said as she grabbed a blanket to cover herself.

"It's no problem," Josh said as he began to gather his clothes. "I'll call you."

Josh silently put his clothes on and walked out the door. She didn't think it was possible, but Cora felt even worse than before. She picked up her discarded clothes, went to her room and shut the door. She cried on her bed in the darkened room. Why did loving someone hurt so much?

Cora stayed in her apartment on Sunday. She turned off her phone and spent the day reading a novel. In the evening, she packed for her trip to her grandmother's. She had one week left at Locke Inc. and Brent would be out of the office until Friday. Avoiding him would be simple. She wasn't going to talk to Josh either. She needed time to evaluate her life and find herself. She couldn't wait to have time with her grandmother. She would know how Cora could move on with her life.

Another week flew by, and suddenly, it was Friday – her final day on the job. Unfortunately, Brent was at her desk when she entered the office. She was not happy, and her eyes had no warmth at all for him.

"You sure are good at disappearing," Brent said as he sat in her chair.

"Are you taking over my job? You look rather comfortable at my desk," Cora replied, ignoring his comment.

"You haven't responded to any of my messages."

"My phone is off," Cora simply said.

"I sense a cold front has moved in."

Cora couldn't help but flash a quick smile, "Is it that obvious?"

"Yes, it is," answered Brent in his serious business voice.

"I need some time to sort things out," Cora said as she toyed with a pencil on her desk.

"I will give you time, but we have to talk," Brent said as

he rose up from her chair. His manly scent lingered in the air as he walked off to his office and shut the door. Cora knew that conversation would never happen. As difficult as it would be, she would have to cut him out of her life. He simply was not available; regardless of how she felt toward him. He had a beautiful wife and family to love. In time, hopefully she would find that too.

Brent remained distant the rest of the day. It was a horrible way to spend their last time together. At the end of the day, Cora hugged her co-workers and promised to stay in touch. Brent did not come out to say goodbye. Cora went up to his office, drew her hand in a fist to knock on the door, but she just couldn't do it. It tore her apart, but she needed to let him go, and so she turned and left without a final good-bye. She was done.

Chapter 12

The following day, Julie picked Cora up at her apartment at 7am to take her to the airport. They chatted about work and life. Cora began perking up thinking about her trip. She couldn't wait to see her grandmother.

"Cora, enjoy yourself. You've been so serious lately. It is unlike you. I'll pick you up next Saturday at 3pm. Just wait outside the baggage claim area," Julie called out to Cora.

"Thank you!" Cora beamed as she walked into the airport.

The flight to New York was relaxing. Cora left her phone off. She wanted a week free of texts, emails and phone calls. It was her time to spend with one of the most important people in her life. When she was with her grandmother, she didn't have to worry about a thing. Cora was loved and easily returned the love. It was absolutely wonderful.

After retrieving her luggage, Cora found her grandmother.

"Corina, I can't believe you are here! I have been looking forward to your visit ever since you called. Now, I want to hear all about your generous boss that brought you to me," her grandmother said as she warmly hugged Cora.

"Grandma, there is so much to tell you. I need your advice. I don't know what to do," Cora said as she nuzzled in her grandmother's hair.

"Pumpkin, we will straighten it all out. Don't worry about a thing. Worry only robs us from the joy of the moment. We will take a look at these patterns in your life and find some wiggle room."

"What does that term mean to you?" Cora asked.

"When you look at a something from a different perspective, you find the wiggle room in a situation. This helps you get unstuck and move toward a solution."

"I have missed you so much," Cora said, already feeling better.

"Me, too. I am happy that you could visit. I don't know anything about your boss, but I am thankful that he sent you to me."

"I am too," Cora said wistfully.

They took a cab to her grandmother's condo in New York. The weather was overcast and snow was forecast throughout the Christmas week. All of the stores and

avenues were festive. Store windows displayed
Christmas trees and elegant gifts tantalizing the people
walking by. Cora yearned to tell Brent all about the
amazing day she was having, but she pushed that idea
out of her head. When they reached the condo, Cora
made herself at home in the guest room. Her
grandmother had such class and taste. Her condo was
impeccably decorated, but it also held a warm lived-in
feel to it. Cora loved being there. After taking a
shower and changing into warmer clothes, Cora met
her grandmother in the kitchen.

"Are you ready for dinner, or do you want to talk first?"
her grandmother asked.

"Let's talk," Cora suggested.

Tea and little bread biscuits were out, which was one of
her traditions.

"Now tell me about this generous boss of yours."

"Well, first of all, he is no longer my boss. I have a new
job I will start in a few weeks. A lot has happened
these last few days," Cora said, taking a long sip of her
tea.

"He? Who is 'he'," asked her grandmother.

"Sorry, his name is Brent and he is the CEO of the
Locke family business," Cora said with little interest.

"There is obviously much more to the story. I know
you too well. When you give me only a few details,

there is something brewing underneath. What is it?" her grandmother prodded.

"I don't know where to begin, Grandma. I guess the easiest thing to say is that I have fallen in love with Brent. He is more than I ever wanted. He brings out the best in me and doesn't let me get by with anything, yet at the same time spoils me rotten. He is the first man that I haven't been able to control and run circles around. He is a leader and what a man should be. I can't stop thinking about him. When I am with him, I am so lost in him that all thoughts of right and wrong fly out of my head. Grandma, you would love him, too," Cora said eagerly.

"That was some description! Is he attracted to you and does he feel the same way about you?"

"Yes, we kissed for the first time just days ago. It was magical," Cora whispered.

"I can see that you are taken by him. So what is the problem?"

"He isn't available," Cora said quietly.

"Is that code for the fact that he is married?"

"Yes. He is married to the most beautiful, classy, kind woman I have ever met," Cora said with a sad look on her face.

"I can see the problem."

"I know. I decided that I am going to just cut him out of my life completely," Cora said proudly.

"So you are basically going to run from the situation instead of face it?" her grandmother said with her arms folded across her chest.

"Um…no…. I just don't want to get hurt. I want to walk away from it all."

"Like I just said, you want to hide from it instead of face it. Don't you think you at least owe Brent an explanation?"

"He said he wants to talk. I've been rather elusive with him lately," Cora sheepishly admitted.

"Corina, you aren't being a very good friend. Hiding does not accomplish anything. You need to face your feelings and express yourself to Brent. He has been very kind to you. He deserves the truth. Doesn't he deserve the chance to explain himself? Plus, it will be healing for you as well. If you try and bury your feelings, they won't simply go away. You have to face life head on."

"I am afraid, Grandma. I love him so much. It hurts to see him with his wife. I feel like such a fool," Cora said as tears filled her eyes.

"Come here and give me a hug. There are no failures in life. Wisdom and happiness are not found by running from problems. Cora, I learned a valuable lesson about expressing my feelings instead of ignoring them and my life really turned around. The truth can be painful at first, but it also has a healing quality. I know you don't believe me right now, but you need to talk to Brent."

"I will think about it, I promise. Can we eat now? I am starving," Cora said as her mouth was watering. She hadn't eaten much all day and her stomach was growling.

"Of course; there is a new Italian restaurant down the street. You want to go?"

"Perfect. I could use a hearty meal," Cora said patting her belly.

"I dare say another pound or two would do you some good. Let's go fatten you up," her grandmother said as she pinched Cora's side.

"Funny. I will go grab my purse."

Cora and her grandmother had a great dinner. They shared some funny stories about daily life and kept the conversation light. Her grandmother knew not to press Cora on an issue. She needed time to marinate and think things over.

The next few days were full of Christmas activities. They went to the mall and joined the other frenzied shoppers. Her grandmother wanted to catch a movie and eat popcorn with tons of butter. They even watched the ice skaters in Central Park. On Christmas Eve, they attended the midnight candlelight service. It was so peaceful. The service was a subtle reminder of how far Cora had gotten away from God. She had been so busy running her own life that she forgot to stop and ask God for help. When the room was dark and her candle was lit, she paused to say a prayer for guidance in her life. After her prayer, she felt a weight lift off her heart. She knew it would all be okay, regardless of the result. Life was about more than getting what you wanted. It was about being thankful for what you had and remembering to live in possibility.

On Christmas Day, Cora woke up to a fresh blanket of snow covering New York City. The snow reminded her of the trip she took to Glacier National Park and her revelations about her relationship with Josh. Cora had spoken to her grandmother often regarding her feelings toward Josh. Her grandmother listened, but did not offer any advice. She merely shook her head and patted Cora's hand.

Cora filled her coffee cup and went to her purse to find her phone. She had purposefully left it off during her trip. She wanted time away from everyone. It felt like she had a small measure of control over a very confusing situation. However, it was Christmas. She turned on her phone. There were several emails from Josh. Cora didn't feel like reading those. There was one voicemail from Brent. Cora punched in her password and listened to the message,

"Merry Christmas, Corina. I've been trying to connect with you. Apparently, your phone is off. I hope you are doing okay. It would be really great to talk to you today. Please call me if you can."

It felt incredible to hear Brent's voice. Cora replayed the message over and over again so she could hear his voice. She melted when he called her Corina. Cora wasn't sure if she should contact him. She wanted to talk to him, but she also needed to cut him out of her life. Yet he sounded worried about her.

"Corina, are you alright? You look sad," Cora's grandmother said as she hugged Cora.

"Oh, Grandma, I am really confused. I checked my phone messages and there was a call from Brent." Cora played the message for her grandmother.

"Well, what did you say when you called him back?"

"What? I haven't called him. You think I should call him?" Cora was completely unsure of what to do.

"Sweetheart, you need to make that decision yourself."

"I am so confused. On one hand, I desperately want to talk to him because I have such strong feelings for him. But I also know that I am only going to end up hurt, so I want to run away from it all," Cora said as she bit her nails.

"It's time to stop running, Corina, and face your fears," Cora's grandmother told her tenderly.

"I'm just avoiding the end. By putting off our conversation, I can stay in the fantasy that it is not completely done and that there is hope for us," Cora admitted.

"Corina, that is what I am talking about. If you face the truth, it will help you sort it all out. The longer you wait to have that conversation with Brent, the more anxiety you will drag around with you."

"Thank you, Grandma. You always know exactly what to say. I'll take the first step and go contact him. I love you."

"I love you too, Corina. Merry Christmas."

"Merry Christmas," Cora said as she walked out of the room. Cora decided against speaking directly to Brent, as her nerves were raw. Instead, she settled on texting him,

'Merry Christmas Brent! It was good to hear your voice. I am having a wonderful time with my grandmother, thanks to your generosity. When I return, I hope to be ready to have that talk.'

Cora sent the text and put her phone back in her purse. She spent the rest of the day focused on her grandmother. They exchanged presents and went on a walk in the snow. They prepared a Christmas feast at home and watched "It's a Wonderful Life." Before she went to bed, Cora checked her phone and there was a one-word text message from Brent.

It simply read, 'Ok.'

Cora laughed. The man got straight to the point.

The following morning, Cora shared a dream she had during the night with her grandmother.

"Grandma, I had the most interesting dream last night. I was given a golden key with the number 47 on it. A voice told me that the key would unlock my destiny. There were several locked doors in front of me. I picked a door, put in my golden key and it unlocked. As I opened the door, I was greeted by a beautiful woman who told me there is only love, faith and hope. If I kept my heart open and full of gratitude, I would live a life glowing with grace," Cora said, still enthralled in the magical feeling of the dream.

"Grandma, I have always believed that we all come into this world with possible destinies and I believe we create our destiny with our choices. I have always wanted the destiny of love. What do you think the 47 represents?"

Grandma sipped her coffee slowly and lovingly said, "I definitely believe that love is your destiny, Corina." Cora's grandmother looked peaceful as she pondered her thoughts.

"Honey, real love involves growth. This world tests us all through our personal life to find out if our motives are aligned. It tests our strength, our willpower and our capacity to be unstoppable in the face of difficult times and not run away. We all have our share of challenges. In time, the storm passes and the sunny sky is revealed. But a lot of people come to this stage with selfish motives to get something for themselves such as personal power, wealth, and sex, instead of giving their love. Many people get stuck in this selfish stage and never get past it."

"If you really want to love someone, you must first love yourself. If you really love and respect yourself, the love you feel for the other person will not have strings or conditions. Real love allows the other person to be true to their own self, which means accepting them for exactly how they are without trying to change them," she went on.

"As for the number 47, I can share with you that when I attended college in Claremont, California in the 1960's, the number 47 was very significant to the students and faculty. Supposedly, a student or professor there completed a mathematical proof that showed all numbers were equal to 47. Since then, students have been quietly compiling evidence that shows how, when chosen randomly, the number 47 appears more often than any other number. The students concluded that it isn't a random occurrence. Perhaps your dream suggests you have 47 possible destinies. But maybe your best possible destiny is to live from your heart and abandon your doubts and fears."

Cora was amazed at how cool it was to experience her grandmother opening up and fully expressing herself. While some of it sounded a little hocus-pocus, she got what she needed. It was time for Cora to face her fear of love and move on with her life. Cora and her grandma were energized and smiling from ear to ear, and their eyes twinkled as they hugged and told each other, "I love you!"

The next few days were a blur. Cora and her grandmother made the most of their time together. On their way to the airport, Cora's grandmother gave her one last nugget:

"Remember, there are no problems in life, only patterns of energy appearing as our life conditions. Problems are fixed and stuck. If you look at just your problem, you will stay stuck. Problems always have some wiggle room in them or other possibilities. If you look and are open to finding new possibilities, you will find the opportunities for change. Find that wiggle room and see the possibilities. All successful people do this. Don't run away from life. I love you, Corina."

"Wow Grandma! Thank you for that inspiration! I love you so much," Cora said, as she began to cry.

It was difficult to say goodbye, but there was a lot back home for her to tackle. She had a little over one week before she began her new job. Plus now she made a commitment to call Brent, have the dreaded discussion, and move forward with her life.

Chapter 13

Cora's flight back to San Francisco was smooth. She took a short nap and enjoyed the in-flight movie. Upon arrival at the San Francisco airport, she retrieved her luggage and then walked outside of the baggage claim area as Julie had instructed. Cora's flight was on time, so Julie would likely be waiting outside. She couldn't wait to tell her all about her trip. It would be nice to have some girl time to decompress.

While Cora was looking for Julie's car, a black Audi pulled up next to her. Brent stepped out of the vehicle, took Cora's bags and put them in his trunk. He opened the passenger side door.

"Ready to go?" Brent asked, as Cora was frozen in place from the shock of Brent unexpectedly meeting her at the airport.

"Julie is picking me up. I am waiting for her," Cora said, dumbfounded.

Saying this, her heart was instantly stirred as she almost forgot how handsome he was, especially in his casual clothes. It was the first time she had seen him in shorts. Oh my, they fit him perfectly. His tight, muscular legs were driving her crazy. She did not trust herself alone around this man as her "Got to Be Strong Mantra" left her completely.

"Cora, I told Julie that I would pick you up. She isn't coming for you," Brent said with no emotion.

"Oh. Ok, I guess," Cora said as she slowly got into the car.

The ride back into the city was quiet. Neither Brent nor Cora spoke a word. There was no music playing, so Cora looked out the window and attempted to gain control over her racing thoughts. Perhaps Julie couldn't make it so she asked Brent to pick her up. He seemed a little bent out of shape, so maybe it was an inconvenient for him to come and get her. She could have taken public transportation or asked Lynn to take off from work. She should have just parked at the airport.

All of the sudden, they were driving over the Golden Gate Bridge and out of the city. They should have been on the Bay Bridge since Cora lived in Berkeley. Where were they going? Cora was too intimidated to ask Brent any questions. She already felt terrible that she put him out. It was Saturday and she was taking time away from his kids.

Brent turned off Highway 101 onto Highway 1. It was a crisp, clear, sunny day as they rode along the scenic highway toward the ocean. Brent's expression was stoic. Cora was uncomfortable. She still had no idea where he was taking her, but was beginning not to care.

The views of the large redwoods were nice. After driving through the trees, the ocean appeared. There must have been no wind outside as there were hardly any whitecaps. The longer they drove, the less Cora wanted to speak. She just surrendered to being near Brent and remaining in the fantasy. She knew the pending talk would come at some point in the day and ultimately end this dream, yet she was in no hurry to get there.

Cora's demeanor improved as they passed through the town of Bodega Bay. She loved the quaint town with the small library, community center and taffy shop. It was a small sea town with enormous character. Fishing boats bobbed up and down by the docks while others meandered around the bay. It was mid-afternoon and several sightseers were making the most of the gorgeous weather.

Cora went to Bodega Bay several times a year. When she was listless, she would often drive out to Bodega Bay to purchase crabs or have some clam chowder at a local restaurant. A few times, she went to the book sale that was held in the community center. She scored quite a few older books and magazines at the last sale. She resisted sharing this little story with Brent, as he was completely lost in his own world.

After passing through town, Brent exited the highway on the ocean side. He took a small road that ended at a large wooden beach house. The house was straight out of a magazine. It was two stories, with decks on both levels. The outside décor was simple and wood adorned everything. There were trees sculpted by the wind at the back of the house, which added privacy and shade to the already secluded location. The front part of the property was wide-open, full of native grasslands. Dotted throughout the native plants were patches of wildflowers and ice plant. The grasses ended at a cliff where the ocean lay below with roaring waves.

Brent pulled into the garage and parked. He got out of the car and opened Cora's door. Continuing to go along with Brent, Cora was not sure where she was.

Just then, Brent announced, "Welcome to my house. Would you like to use the restroom before we go on our walk?"

"Yes. Thank you." Cora was glad he asked. Her bladder was filled to the brim, but she didn't want to mention it.

Cora hoped this was a second home, his beach house and not the home he shared Grace and the kids. Cora followed Brent out of the garage and through the door that led into the kitchen. The house was magnificent. The kitchen flowed into the living room and the outside was brought inside. Wood abounded: wooden floors, trim, moulding, cabinets, and furniture. Where there wasn't wood, there was glass. The views were indescribable. A large wooden deck spanned the front part of the house with an elaborate staircase leading down to the ocean. Vases held fresh lavender, and were sprinkled all over the house.

"Would you like to see the upstairs?" Brent asked.

"Don't tell me there's more," Cora said taking it all in.

"Most homes have at least one bedroom where people sleep," Brent jokingly stated.

The stairway leading up to the second floor was airy and open. It wasn't closed-in, like traditional homes. Everything about the house was customized and elegantly unique. While it wasn't constructed in a modern sense, it had special touches that weren't often found in a home by the beach. The upstairs contained even more glass than the first level. At the top of the stairs was a large sitting room filled with comfortable chairs and numerous bookshelves filled with a variety of books. Cora wanted to peruse the titles, but Brent was watching her every move. Each bedroom wall facing the outdoors was glass from floor to ceiling. Cora trailed Brent into all of the rooms. She soaked it all in without asking any questions. Since she was with Brent, she resisted the temptation to touch anything. The second level also contained a large deck, which wrapped all the way around the house. The areas to take in the view were limitless. She was so enthralled with the tour of the house and so far she had not seen any signs of Grace and his children.

"The bathroom is on the left," Brent said.

"Thank you," Cora said as she made her way to the bathroom. When she came out, Brent was nowhere to be found in any of the rooms. Cora walked around a little more and was impressed with the simplicity of the furnishings; yet it all was done with such class. There was a refreshing peace in the house, which overcame her as she walked from room to room. Clutter was not to be found and Cora wondered if anyone actually lived there. However, each room had fresh flowers by the bedside. Cora made her way to the master bedroom. A large wooden king-sized bed filled the room. She wanted to dive in the decorative pillows, but remained in control. The view from the master bedroom faced due west. The sunset views were undoubtedly perfect. The room was large enough for a sliding glass door out to the deck. Cora could only imagine what it must feel like to wake up to the sun coming in the window or watch the fog creep over the ocean and up onto the land.

When she had finished looking at the bedrooms, she took the stairs back to the first floor. He looked striking, like he was right out of a GQ magazine. Cora's heart skipped a beat. She gathered her composure and met him outside.

"Done snooping?" Brent inquired. "I hope you didn't break anything."

"I didn't touch a thing," Cora shot back.

"Even the books? I saw you eyeing those."

"If I am so untrustworthy, why did you leave me up there by myself?"

"I wanted to give you time to come to your own conclusions," Brent said mysteriously.

"About what?" Cora asked.

"Whether or not you like my house," Brent said as he smiled at her.

"Is this really your house?"

"Did you think I just rented a house on the ocean for our talk?"

"No. I thought maybe it belonged to your family as a vacation home," Cora said, yet again astounded by the man.

"This is my home, Cora. I enjoy this home and the energy of this area," Brent said as he turned away. "Let's take a walk. It is time for our talk."

Brent led the way down the stairs to the beach. At the bottom of the stairs was another large deck. Brent pointed to some chairs and they sat down.

"Would you like to begin or shall I?" Brent asked.

"I would like to start. I need to just get this all out. Please don't interrupt me. It has taken me time and a lot of courage to formulate what I want to say. Okay?"

"Okay, I promise not to speak," Brent said as he sat back in his chair.

"When I first met you, I thought you were the most irritating, intolerable, and pompous man I have ever met. As I have gotten to know you better, I have realized that you are the true definition of a man:

246

competent, strong, capable, and a leader. I am incredibly attracted to that part of you, but even more so to who you are inside."

"When I am with you, I am happy. You are so fun to be with and you make feel really good and confident. You have stirred within me so many thoughts and feelings. I am more myself when I am with you than I have even been. This is all new for me. I have caught glimpses of myself throughout my life, but never has it all flowed together like it does when we are together."

"Everything has converged together for me and it is truly beautiful. It is like preparing for a huge conference event. You work on all the pieces separately. You have a plan of how everything will turn out on the day of the big event, but you can't ever quite fully envision it until it happens. You celebrate the accomplishments along the way of putting it together. However, until the big day comes, it is still unclear. But oh, when it does come, it is simply amazing. You stand back in awe and are stunned by how truly beautifully intricate it all is. That is exactly how I feel around you. All of these different parts of me are coming together at once and I am amazed that it is all me. It has been quite a revelation," Cora said as she sat back in the chair. Brent reached over and held her hand. As instructed, he didn't say a word.

"I have finally found not only the man I want to be with, but also the truest version of myself and I need to let it all go. As much as I want to act on my heart and my feelings for you, I cannot. I need to say goodbye and walk away. I cannot live in this fantasy world any longer. I hope you understand." Cora said as she pulled back her hand and stood up to face the ocean. She didn't want Brent to see her cry again.

"I don't understand," Brent said in a serious tone. "I have been so used to being alone within myself. It bothers me that when we are apart, I want you with me. You carry this fire within yourself that drives me wild. I have shown you parts of myself that I don't usually share. It is easy and fun with you. And now you are just walking away without even giving me an explanation? I will not allow it to end like this, Corina. Tell me why."

"You want to hear the words? Fine. I refuse to be the one to come between you, Grace and your kids," Cora cried out.

"Me and Grace? Kids? What does any of this have to do with Grace and the kids?" Brent said, totally lost and confused by Cora's explanation.

"It has everything to do with your wife!" Cora stated in a raised voice.

As Brent finally caught on to what Cora had incorrectly convinced herself about him, he could not contain his laughter. Cora, not knowing the truth, did not feel it was funny and became overwhelmed.

Cora angrily yelled, "I am so done with you Brent Locke and I never want to see you again! I knew I should have never trusted you and come here today with you!"

"Cora, wait. I am sorry. Please wait," Brent called out as he ran after her. Cora did not stop. The tears were falling now and there was no stopping them. Brent caught up to her and wrestled her to the ground. Cora tried to fight him off of her, but it was no use.

Brent gently kissed her cheek and whispered in her ear, "I am not married. I have never been married, Corina." Cora was beyond shocked.

"I don't understand. Your mother told me that you were the perfect family. I have seen Grace's wedding ring, your children, and how much you love the children. You look so happy when you are together," Cora said, searching Brent's eyes for an explanation.

"Grace Locke is not my wife; she is my brother's wife and now his widow, and the children are theirs. She is like a little sister to me. Yes, she is a beautiful woman, but I don't have any romantic feelings for her. Another more beautiful woman has taken my heart. Her name is Corina Jacobs. Do you know her?"

Cora's face was now a wet mixture of sand and tears. Was she daydreaming again? Did she really just hear Brent tell her that he wasn't married?

"Brent, I don't understand. You aren't married to Grace?"

"Cora, I am not married to Grace. I have no intention of marrying Grace, much to my mother's dismay," Brent said with a huge smile on his face. "I am in love with you."

"What did you just say?" Cora couldn't fathom what he just said.

"Sweetheart, are you alright? You look so pale," Brent asked, concerned that Cora looked completely out of it.

"Your mother had me believing that you were married. She does not like me and lied to me," Cora said, tears streaming down her cheeks.

"She is afraid of my feelings you, Corina. She sees the way I look at you and she knows that I have fallen in love with you," Brent said as he stroked Cora's cheek and wiped the sand from her face. "I love you, Cora," said Brent.

"And, I love you too, Brent," Cora said, now with happier tears and a huge smile, shaking her head saying over and over, "I just can't believe this!"

"Baby, you mean so much to me. I have waited a long time to tell you how I feel. We would get really close and then you would pull away from me. I thought it was because of Bruce. I know, I know, ok, Josh. But, he was never the one for you," Brent lovingly told Cora.

Then he added, "I was also concerned about how the other employees at the office would treat you if they knew about my feelings. I didn't want your career to be in jeopardy because of me. I talked to my dad about my concerns. He came up with the idea of getting you a promotion and raise at another company in what seemed like a win-win solution. Then he went and made it happen by promoting you and your excellent work skills to his business colleagues. There was more than one company interested in hiring you. I hope you don't mind his interference. He is infatuated with you. I guess he figures if he can't have you, then at least he can have you in the family."

"I love your dad!" Cora said laughing at Brent's description of his dad. "I can't wait to start my new job."

"I am very happy to hear that, Cora. I was concerned that he might have gone a little too far."

"No, it was kind of you both to think about my career. I should focus on that more myself," Cora said, still trying to take it all in.

"I want to show you something," Brent said as he helped her off the sand. Cora brushed herself off and took a look around. "The land as far as you can see belongs to me. I come out here a lot to gather my thoughts. Lately, all of my thoughts have been of you. I've wanted to bring you out here so many times. You won't see anyone out here for miles. It is very peaceful. I am glad I can share it with you."

As they walked out closer to the ocean, everything seemed right in the world. He guided her closer to the water, toward the rocks. He found a long flat rock and pressed her down upon it. He gently laid his jacket beneath her head as she gazed up at him. He lifted up her dress and slipped off her panties. Brent knelt down beside her in the sand and slowly pushed her thighs apart. As he bent his head down, he caressed the inside of her thighs with the side of his face, sending waves of love straight to her heart.

As he teased her toes, calves and the back of her knees and thighs, the warmth of his hands and the knowledge of what he was about to do next nearly split her apart. His eyes locked with hers for one brief moment before he took what already belonged to him. His mouth moved across her in a slow, methodical roll. It moved around…and around…and around. He told her to feel the rolling of the waves in concert with his tongue to set her orgasms with the crashing of the waves. The intensity overtook all of her senses. She had no choice but to obey. The fresh breeze was cool on her soft behind as the warmth of his mouth caused her juices to release. He kept switching the movements of his tongue back and forth, up and down, round and round until she was dizzy with pleasure.

As she rocked her head back and forth with the motions of his tongue, her gaze swept over to the lights from his house. She turned her head back to her lover and watched as the wind entangled itself with the locks of his hair. Her fingers could not resist joining in the play and wrapped themselves within the softness of each strand. Whenever she felt a jolt of pure lust, she would tug on his hair uniting them both in the feeling. He loved her. There was no longer any doubt. And she loved him with every fiber of her being. As she allowed this realization to penetrate her, pleasure welled inside her and jetted out to her toes and all the way up

her spine. She was complete. She belonged to him.
Fully. And he knew it.

With a devious smile, he pulled her up from the rocks.
He knew they had merged as one. It gave him great
satisfaction to sate her senses and cause her to forget
everything around her. She moved forward in a blissful
state, almost forgetting the need for clothing. She did
not remember her sandals until she felt the rocks brush
against her ankles. She was temporarily helpless and
fully surrendered. She didn't need to concern herself
with anything, he would be her guide her back to his
house.

Her whole body was fresh with excitement by the time
they returned to the house. He challenged her to a race
up the stairs and left her in the dust. His transition
between a man and a little boy happened quickly and
often. When he was really content, he let his guard
down completely and revealed a sensitive, fun, playful
side. It was such a treat to witness this part of him, as
she knew that not many saw this little boy in him. She
could easily imagine his personality at age four as it
showed itself a lot lately when they were together. She
longed to cradle this little boy in her lap and slowly
stroke the little curls which appeared at the nape of his
neck. He was so full of love and life. All he wanted in
life was to love and be loved. It was so easy to do and
be both for him. In fact, nothing brought her more joy
than to do just that.

"Would you like something to eat? Once I get you in
my bed, you will not be leaving it for hours. Consider
yourself warned."

"I am a little hungry after the assault on the beach," Cora said as she slid up next to Brent.

"Come here, baby," Brent said as he pulled her body close to his. He crushed his mouth down on top of hers. After he came up for some air, he let out a sigh. He grabbed a box of crackers and gave it to Cora. "I can't wait another minute. You are going to have to settle on some crackers. I have waited long enough." Brent picked her up and carried her up the stairs to his bedroom.

He laid her down onto his cozy bed. He was done being patient. Their time at the beach had only begun to satisfy the ache they both felt inside. Cora's eyes lit up with excitement when he drew near. She could feel his passion welling up and see its effect in his shorts. He was ready. Brent quickly removed her dress and threw it to the floor. It was not going to be a gentle night. He reached behind her back to wrestle off her bra. As she went to move her hands to help him, the bra was already loose around her breasts. His fingers quickly found her breasts and began to stroke them in a circular motion as he pinched the tip to remind her who was in control; it was definitely not Cora. His other hand was busy caressing her ribs, then her belly and eventually, it landed on her behind. She moaned with pleasure when his hand finally made it to her soft spot.

His eyes moved to hers to gauge her reaction. He enjoyed bringing her right to the edge. She understood him better now and could see further into him. His intensity was reassuring. There was no doubt that he was right there with her in that moment.

Brent took his finger and placed it inside her. His eyes still held hers as he began to move his finger back and forth. At first he was slow. When she grew wetter, he inserted another finger, increasing the speed of the vibrations. The sensations inside her became stronger. When the speed increased, the satisfaction was so overwhelming she almost asked him to stop. By now several pillows had fallen to the floor and her head was flush with the elaborate headboard. She was trapped and excited by it.

"Corina, I know what is best for you," Brent said seductively.

"You do? Why don't you show me then," Cora playfully suggested.

"That is exactly what I am going to do."

"We just have one problem," Cora stated. "You still have all of your clothes on."

"What are you going to do about it?" Brent challenged her.

Cora slowly crawled on top of him and unbuttoned his shorts. They fit him so well, it was almost a shame to remove them. She slid them down his legs and off his feet. She got temporarily distracted when she reached his legs. They were so sculpted and beautiful. Each muscle carried definition and flexed in the perfect places. His skin was a deep warm brown. The sun loved him. He could step outside without his shirt for just minutes and return with a bronze tan. Brent's skin was soft and warm. Before she knew it, her lips were softly licking and kissing his legs. She lost all control. Her fingers ran up and down his body from his waist down to his toes. His eyes were now closed, but she could see his enjoyment in the small smile that escaped from his lips.

It didn't take long for Cora to notice that the bulge was still present. His member was hard and lay flat against him. Black hairs surrounded the space between his legs and each one carried with it a little curl. The hairs felt soft in her fingers as she caressed them. She bent her head down and opened her mouth wide. It was time to return to him some of the ecstasy she had already received. His member slid so smoothly between her lips. It was incredibly soft and had the lightest sweet taste to it. She licked it from the base to the head and back again. The slower she went, the louder he moaned. She enjoyed hearing him moan and seeing him excited by her touch. She felt powerful and in control of the situation, at least for the moment.

Right when she thought he was about to release, Cora suddenly found herself on her back while Brent put on a ribbed condom. He took her forcefully and slid his member deep inside her. It shocked her that he could move so fast. His rhythmic thrusts were hot and tantalizing. His chest brushed against hers and she could feel the tips of her breasts respond to the friction. Her bump rocked against him and caused more juice to escape from her. She was so wet that he almost slipped all the way out of her. She moved her hand around to his back and dug her nails in. She had to hold on, as she was quickly losing control of her body and her mind. She dug her nails down his back, knowing that she would leave marks, but not caring. Cora slapped him once out of sheer excitement and then again because she enjoyed his reaction.

His lips found her ear and he whispered over and over, "Corina, Corina, Corina."

When he said her name, her body shook violently. It brought her to the reality of what was occurring. The man she loved and desired returned her love. It was exhilarating. Their breath was heavy and coming quickly now. She could literally feel the coming together of their spirits.

She couldn't hold on any longer. Another wave began to overtake her. At the height of her orgasm, she felt another storm brewing inside her, but this time it was not her; it was Brent. Every part of her could sense his release right before it happened. The warm little tingles shot all over her and brought another round of new sensations of ecstasy. He let out a moan and released the last drop before he collapsed upon her. They were both drenched in sweat and completely satisfied.

Cora basked in the closeness. As their nude bodies touched closely side by side, she put her head on his chest and listened to the beating of his heart. She felt a spiritual union with him that produced a sense of lightness and belonging. He was in his state of nothingness and she felt victorious. They had made love, more love and passion than either of them had ever known.

Brent placed his right arm around Cora and adoringly stroked her hair with his left hand. It was calming and peaceful, like sitting next to a stream on lush green grass and watching a fallen leaf gently float by.

Brent asked, "Are you hungry, Love?" as he handed Cora a box of crackers.

"Yes, you are quite the host," Cora teased.

"Don't worry, I will feed you. After that session, you deserve a little nutrition."

"Oh good, because I am starving," Cora said, eagerly devouring the snack at hand.

"Let's go downstairs and eat something a little more substantial," Brent said as he pulled on some sweats. He tossed a pair and one of his t-shirts to Cora. "You can put these on for now, if you'd like. I will bring you your suitcases after we eat."

"Thanks," Cora said. It was silly, but Cora was more than happy to wear Brent's clothes. It was like having a part of him with her.

By the time Cora was dressed, Brent was busy in the kitchen. He was pulling various items out of the refrigerator.

"I have a ton of leftovers. Would you like lasagna,

chicken, or fish?" Brent asked as he continued to move things around in the kitchen.

"Lasagna sounds great."

"You sure are looking good in those clothes, Corina! You better eat quickly. I have more plans for you," Brent said, casting Cora a sexy grin.

"It will take me less than three minutes to finish. I will race you back to that big cozy bed of yours," Cora said with raised fork in hand.

"Who said we are going to be in the bed? I have a whole house. In fact, this kitchen counter is pretty sturdy," Brent suggested, as he tested the strength of the counter. It should be able to support you, at least for a short while. Of course if it fails, we always have the kitchen floor."

"Such a clever tease! You better be prepared to deliver," Cora said, as she took the lasagna out of the microwave.

True to her word, she quickly finished her meal. After she was done, she washed her dish and began playing with Brent's hair. She was definitely getting to him, as he had difficulty concentrating on his meal. Cora knelt beside his chair and began to play with the string on his sweat pants. Brent pushed his chair from the table, stood up and pulled down the pants he had just given her to wear very slowly. They continued their lovemaking in the kitchen, until Brent scooped Cora up in his arms and carried her back to his bedroom.

"You should sleep well tonight, Corina," Brent whispered as he tucked her into bed. It was incredibly late and even later for Cora, as she was still on east coast time. Cora quickly drifted off to sleep.

Cora awoke the next morning with a smile as the sun was streaming down on her face. She heard the ocean and gleefully buried herself further under the covers and fluffy pillows. She was so happy, she couldn't contain herself. She was naked in Brent's bed. He loved her. He wasn't married. He wanted to be with her. Cora's head was still spinning from all of these incredible revelations. Brent. Just the mention of his name got her. He was an unbelievable lover.

"Top of the afternoon!" Brent bellowed out as he ripped the covers off the bed, startling Cora.

"You are such a brute! And here I was just lying here thinking about how wonderful you are. Ha!" Cora replied as she folded her arms across her chest.

"Are you going to sleep all day? It's already past noon," Brent said as he pointed to the clock.

Cora began to argue until she saw the clock. It was 12:35pm. "I rarely sleep this late," Cora blushed, embarrassed by the time.

"We had quite the workout last night," Brent said as he began sucking on Cora's toes.

"You can say that again," Cora said as she fell back into

the pillows.

Brent moved from Cora's toes, up her calves, over her thighs and then went to work between her legs. He took her up to new heights of pleasure and then let her roll right through them. He was now the master of her body and she was not resisting.

After completely satiating her, Brent led her into the shower. He lathered up the sponge and gently washed her entire body. He said nothing and merely tossed her a smile now and then. Cora let herself go. Brent moved his way around her back and gently slipped himself inside of her. The warmth of the water running down her back combined with the rhythm of Brent against her drove her wild. Brent held on to her hips until he could hold it no longer. He had his release and then nuzzled his head inside Cora's wet hair.

"I sure like the service provided in this shower. I don't think I have ever been cleaner," Cora laughed as she began to wash Brent. She relished seeing him so relaxed.

Brent stepped out of the shower. He took a towel and then fell back into the bed. "I thought we might go into town today, but it seems challenging to make it out of the house," Brent laughed.

"I feel great! Once you recover, we can go into town," Cora said as she dried off. Brent had brought in her suitcase so she was able to change into her own clothes. She noticed that her dirty clothes were missing.

"Your other clothes are in the dryer," Brent said as he pulled the pillow off his face.

"How do you always seem to know what I am thinking?" Cora asked, puzzled that he was usually correct.

"You would be a terrible poker player. It all shows on your face. I must correct you, though, if I always knew what you were thinking, we would have been together months ago," Brent said as he got up and began to dress.

"Good point. However, if you would have told me that the picture on your desk is your niece and nephew when I asked about them, your mother's lie would have been easily avoided," Cora said as she playfully swiped at Brent with a pillow.

"If you would have come down and met Grace when we were at The Del, there would have been no misunderstanding," Brent said as he flashed her a smile and grabbed the pillow out of her hand.

"I am just glad the truth came out," Cora said lovingly as she pulled Brent back into bed.

In the early evening, Brent asked Cora, "What are your plans for the next week?"

"I don't have any. I have been so busy lately that I was just going to hang out around my apartment. I have a week before my new job starts."

"Perfect. Tomorrow morning, I will drive you to your apartment so you can pack for our trip," Brent said without any further details.

"Pack? Where are we going?" Cora was very excited to go anywhere with Brent.

"It's a surprise. We will leave tomorrow afternoon and be back on Sunday. You will need a dress for each evening and a special party dress for New Year's Eve. Be sure to bring your swimsuit and also an ample amount of day clothes. The weather is similar to here, if not a bit warmer. Got it?" Brent said, making sure he covered everything without giving away the destination. "One more thing: I know you will love it there!"

Chapter 14

The next day, their flight arrived in San Diego. Not seeing any evidence of a connecting flight to another location, Cora was happy to be back in San Diego with Brent. She was hopeful that they would stay at the Hotel del Coronado. She tried to put it out of her mind. She was with Brent and that was all that mattered. A car picked them up at the airport and drove them out toward the island. As they drove over the Coronado Bridge, Cora flashed Brent a huge smile.

"I knew that you would be happy to return here. It was at the Hotel Del Coronado that I fell in love with you and now that we are together, I want to enjoy it as a couple." Brent said as he leaned over to kiss her.

Cora beamed at Brent and laid her head on his shoulder. As they were driving through the town of Coronado, her attention was riveted on all the various shops and restaurants they passed. The local coffee shop was still humming into the evening. The boutiques all wore fancy 'Closed' signs as it was way past time to buy beachwear or bedazzling flip-flops. As the shops passed by, she placed her hand out the window to grasp the warm summer air. Feeling sentimental, again she wanted seal this happy experience into her heart. She closed her eyes briefly and breathed it all in.

The Del looked even more enchanting than on her first visit. Cora wasn't sure how that was even possible. Brent reserved the same villa he had stayed in during the conference. It was all a dream come true.

"Corina, you have no idea how many times during our conference I wanted to bring you to this villa and show you how I felt. You were driving me absolutely crazy. I wanted you. I watched your every move that week. You glided around with such competence and put everyone at ease. My dad was practically falling all over himself to have time with you. I knew exactly how he felt. Now you are here and I have you all to myself. Has there been a luckier man?"

Cora was touched by Brent's ease at expressing himself to her. She finally knew what it was like to love and be loved. She wanted to give everything to this man, the very best of herself.

The next day was New Year's Eve. Brent made Cora a reservation at the spa. She was in heaven. She ordered the deep tissue package that included full body rejuvenation. She felt like a princess.

Throughout her day, she began to think about the different sensations she felt when they were together. She could feel the coolness of his bedroom and the light scent of him, which it held. The memory of the soft texture of his sheets brought shivers on her arms. The incredibly soft pillows that he adored made her smile by just thinking of them.

He wanted to make her happy: spoil her, play, have fun, live. He did all that and more. Her head was spinning, unable to capture everything they had experienced. They were on life's shopping spree: tasting, feeling, seeing and living all they could possibly imagine or create.

In her past relationships, the images in her mind or her hidden expectations often fell short of reality. Yet with Brent, it was so different. The energy they sustained as individuals combined with their collective energy as a couple brought out the best in both of them. Cora was hopelessly in love.

When she was finished at the spa, she returned to find Brent grinning from ear to ear.

"Did you enjoy yourself?" Brent asked sweetly.

"I doubt I have ever been this relaxed. Thank you."

"Are you ready for your Christmas present?" Brent said eagerly.

"Christmas present? But it is New Year's Eve. I didn't get you anything for Christmas," Cora said, feeling bad that she didn't bring him a present. Granted, last week she didn't think she would see him ever again, but that wasn't a good reason. Was it?

"I can see the wheels in your head are turning like crazy. Let me try again. I have a surprise for you.

Close your eyes."

Cora complied and closed her eyes. She heard a little shuffling and wondered what the man was doing.

"Ok, you can open your eyes."

Cora opened her eyes and saw a little box wrapped in gold paper with red velvet ribbon.

"It's too beautiful to open," gushed Cora.

"We can keep it wrapped," Brent deviously suggested.

"No way. I want to know what is inside," Cora said as she ripped off the paper. She opened the box to find a delicate pair of diamond earrings.

"I wanted to start the New Year out right. You dazzled me last year when you came into my life and I can't wait for this year ahead with you, Corina."

The Del was hosting a New Year's Eve ball. The decorations from Christmas were still proudly displayed throughout the hotel. Cora chose a long white gown from a shop in town that fit her like a glove. She straightened her hair so it was smooth as silk. She wore her new diamond earrings. As she was putting on the last few touches of her make-up, Brent nuzzled up behind her.

"Corina, you look exquisite," he said nibbling on her ear.

"Thank you," Cora cooed back at him.

"Are you ready, my love?" Brent said as he took her arm in his.

"I am," Cora said after she put on her lipstick.

"How about we take the long way over to the ball and catch the sunset?"

They walked together on the path beside the ocean. While it was amazingly picturesque, none of it compared to the contentment she felt deep within. With every glance at him, the love she felt for him shot straight through her again. The jolt of it rocked her and continually surprised her, for a dreamer to find contentment is rare.

As they continued on the path, he shifted his hand and began to slowly caress her wrist with his thumb. His fingers moved in a slow dance with her palm and then they traveled up her arm and back down again.
Brent stopped when they reached the spot where Kate Morgan had died. He paused and looked at Cora.

"What was it like?" he asked.

"What like?" Cora questioned, unsure of what Brent meant.

"Were you afraid the night you saw Kate?"

"No. I was very upset that night. I think she came to comfort me."

"Why were you upset?" Brent asked tenderly.

"It was the night of the luau. Your mother and I were talking on the beach. She said that you and Grace made the perfect family. I saw you dancing with Grace; her wedding band twinkled in the lights. I was shocked and saddened. It is why I left The Del early. I couldn't handle seeing you again. I also fell in love with you that week at The Del."

"Sweetheart, I am so sorry my mother led you to believe that lie. Let me hold you," Brent said, wanting to make up for the undue pain caused by the deceit. Cora didn't care about it anymore. She was so utterly happy that it just didn't matter. She understood Brent's mother probably wanted him to be with Grace, but she also knew his dad really liked Cora with Brent.

"Brent, I am fine. You know when your dad told me about the job offer, he said that it was my destiny. I don't think he was just referring to the job, was he?"

"Am I your destiny, Cora?" Brent inquired.

"Yes, Brent. You are absolutely my destiny," Cora said as they embraced and passionately began kissing.

After sharing maybe their longest and sweetest kiss, Cora gazed up at The Del. Much to her surprise, she saw something move in one of the windows. In her heart, she knew it was Kate. She was excited.

"Brent, Kate is watching us! Don't look right away, but

if you turn your eyes slowly to the left, you will see her up in the window. Can you see her?" Cora asked quietly.

"I can," Brent whispered back.

The three of them stared at each other in silence, not knowing what to expect. Brent slowly pulled Cora closer to his side. Kate looked at them and a small smile formed on her lips. Then she disappeared.

"Was that my imagination or did she smile at us?" Cora asked.

"Maybe she can sense how much I love you," Brent said, gazing lovingly at Cora.

"I love you too, Brent Locke. You are like the sunset I am experiencing this very minute: breathtaking, expansive, magical, illuminating, ever changing, and at this very moment, mine to love. I know that I can share anything with you and this means everything to me," Cora said, full of love.

"Acceptance is a rare gift and love is even better. I know that I have both in you and for you. My heart is brimming with love for you, and I have never, never felt this good. Cora, I am so grateful for your love and I know that with you, anything is possible," Brent said adoringly.

Cora responded, "I cannot help but wonder where my life will take me. Wherever it leads, you must know that you will forever go with me. You have become a part of my life in so many different ways," Cora said as she reached for his hand.

Cora and Brent walked together as joyful and loving souls. Their hearts had merged as one and their journey to find their destinies was complete. True love was their destiny.

Note from author: If you didn't want this story to end, please write a review at www.amazon.com.